POKÉMON

ASH'S QUEST
THE ESSENTIAL GUIDEBOOK

BY SIMCHA WHITEHILL

SCHOLASTIC INC.

All rights reserved. Published by Scholastic Inc., *Publishers since 1920*. SCHOLASTIC and associated logos are trademarks and/or registered trademarks of Scholastic Inc.

The publisher does not have any control over and does not assume any responsibility for author or third-party websites or their content.

ISBN 978-1-338-31517-2

10 9 8 7 6 5 4 3 2 1   19 20 21 22 23

Printed in China   62
First printing 2019

Book design by Kay Petronio and Carolyn Bull

CONTENTS

INTRODUCTION

Have you ever wondered what it would be like to be a Pokémon Trainer traveling from region to region, challenging Gym Leaders for badges, catching wild Pokémon, competing in tournaments, and spotting Legendary Pokémon along the way?

Now's your chance to find out! In this book, you'll travel through Kanto, Johto, Hoenn, Sinnoh, Unova, Kalos, and Alola with one of the greatest Pokémon Trainers of all time: Ash Ketchum. This ten-year-old boy is following his dream of becoming a Pokémon Master. His quest has been filled with action, adventure, friends, foes, and amazing Pokémon battles. And now he's inviting YOU to join him on his journey!

Are you ready for adventure? Then what are you waiting for? Turn the page!

MEET ASH

Ash is a ten-year-old boy on a mission to become a Pokémon Master. It is a dream he's dedicated his life to. Ash is always fighting the good fight, no matter what the circumstances. Look out, bullies and villains—Ash isn't afraid to stand up for what he believes in. Whether Team Rocket attacks or a wild Pokémon goes on a rampage, Ash is there to save the day—with the help of his Pokémon pals and travel buddies, of course.

To Ash, being a good Trainer is all about building the friendship between him and his Pokémon. Nothing is too big a challenge, because they can handle anything as a team. It's no wonder so many Trainers, Coordinators, Connoisseurs, and Pokémon have been inspired to join him on his journey.

In this book, you'll get to travel with Ash and all his friends—Pokémon and people alike. So let's follow Ash from the place where it all began, a little place called Pallet Town in the Kanto region.

PIKACHU

One pal has been right by Ash's side since he began his journey—Pikachu.
This little Electric-type is so independent, it refuses to travel inside a
Poké Ball like most Pokémon do. But although it's strong-willed, Pikachu
knows nothing is stronger than the bond of friendship it shares with its
best friend, Ash. Together, they have traveled near and far, won countless
battles, and foiled many an evil plot. They are an unstoppable team!

Pikachu is known to shock its opponents on the battlefield—literally!
Its amazing attacks include Electro Ball, Thunder, Thunder Shock, and
Thunderbolt.

You might want to pinch those cute, round cheeks, but it's electricity that
keeps them so cute and puffy. So beware of getting zapped!

ASH AND PIKACHU'S STORY

HOW DID ASH AND PIKACHU'S STORY BEGIN? READ ON TO FIND OUT!

Ash was lying in his bed in Pallet Town, but he couldn't sleep. He was too excited! The next day he would finally get to meet his first partner Pokémon at Professor Oak's lab.

The ten-year-old Trainer was glued to his TV, where Professor Oak was explaining the three Pokémon he'd get to choose from: Bulbasaur, Charmander, and Squirtle.

Knock-knock! Ash's mom, Delia, opened the door to his bedroom.

"Ash, time to turn off the television. You need a good night's rest for tomorrow," she said.

Ash hugged his mom good night and set his Poké Ball alarm clock. Then he closed his eyes. The faster he fell asleep, the faster morning would come.

But in Ash's dream, his chance to pick a first partner Pokémon had already come. He was at Professor Oak's lab, and he grabbed a Poké Ball—except it was really his alarm clock!

"Squirtle, I choose you!" cheered Ash, tossing it.

Smash! His alarm clock hit the wall and broke into bits. The new Trainer stayed fast asleep.

Luckily, the next morning, the sun's bright rays woke Ash. When he spotted his broken clock, he cried, "Oh, no—I'm going to be late for my first day as a Pokémon Trainer!"

Ash hurried out the door in his pajamas. He ran all the way to Professor Oak's lab, arriving just as his rival, Gary Oak, was leaving.

"Nice outfit," Gary sneered.

"Did you already choose your first partner Pokémon?" Ash asked.

"Yep, and I got the best one," Gary said. "It helps when your grandfather is the top professor in Kanto."

"Which one did you choose?" Ash asked.

"Ha! Like I'd tell a loser like you," Gary replied.

"Someday I'm going to be a Pokémon Master!" Ash promised.

"Yeah, right, you can't even make it on time to get your first Pokémon," Gary said.

Ash ran up the steps to the lab, where he was greeted by Professor Oak.

"I choose Squirtle!" Ash proclaimed.

But Ash was so late that Bulbasaur, Charmander, and Squirtle were all gone. There was only one Pokémon left—a bright-yellow Pikachu with big red cheeks. Professor Oak warned Ash that there was a problem with it.

"Aw," said Ash, hugging his adorable new friend. "What could be wrong with this cute Pikachu?"

"*Piiiiikkkkaaaaachuuuuuuu!*" the Electric-type screamed, zapping Ash.

"Well, uh, good luck on your journey!" Professor Oak said, handing Ash his Pokédex and six Poké Balls.

Ash was a little fried from his new friend's powerful jolt of electricity, but he was still excited about starting out. If only Pikachu was just as excited . . . but it wouldn't go into its Poké Ball! Every time Ash tossed it, Pikachu whacked it back with its tail. So Ash decided to carry Pikachu. But once he picked it up,

Pikachu shocked him again. *Zap!* Finally, the two headed down the road into the forest.

"Pikachu, I've always dreamed of becoming a Pokémon Master, because I love Pokémon!" Ash told the little Electric-type. "I promise I'll be a good friend if you give me the chance."

"*Piiiikaaa,*" Pikachu grumbled.

Just then, a wild Pidgey landed nearby. Ash wanted to try to catch his first Pokémon. It was the perfect chance to win over Pikachu—they'd catch that Pidgey together!

But when Ash shared his plan with Pikachu, the rebellious Electric-type ran up a tree.

"*Pika pika!*" Pikachu taunted.

So Ash decided to try to catch Pidgey on his own. He took out a Poké Ball and aimed it. Perfect hit!

"*Pidgey!*" the Normal-Flying-type squawked as it went inside the Poké Ball.

"All right!" Ash cheered.

But then the Poké Ball started rocking back and forth. Would it work?

"*Pidgey!*" the Pokémon cried, flying away.

Ash's Pokédex explained that he needed to battle Pidgey to prove himself as a Trainer before he could catch the Pokémon.

"*Pika pika pika!*" Pikachu giggled.

Now Ash was even more determined to catch Pidgey. He tried to sneak up on it and catch it. But Pidgey used Sand Attack to trap Ash in a dirt tornado.

When the dust settled, Ash decided to throw a rock at Pidgey, but he accidentally hit a super-tough Spearow instead. And Spearow wasn't too happy about it.

"*Speeeearow!*" it cried, speeding toward Ash.

Ash quickly dodged the Pokémon's attack. But once Spearow spotted

Pikachu up in the tree, it swooped in to knock down the Electric-type.

"*Pikaaaaaa!*" Pikachu cried, running back and forth.

"Hey, leave Pikachu alone! It didn't throw the rock," Ash shouted.

Pikachu slipped. It was hanging off the tree branch!

"Oh, no, Pikachu!" Ash cried.

There was only one thing to do. When Spearow swooped in again, Pikachu zapped it with its powerful charge! Spearow and Pikachu both landed safely on the ground, but now the battle had begun in earnest.

"*Spearooooooow!*" the Normal-Flying-type cried. Suddenly, the sky was filled with a flock of angry Spearow. They were heading straight for Ash and Pikachu!

"Run!" Ash told Pikachu.

The two raced through the woods, but the Spearow were close behind.

"Don't worry, Pikachu. No matter what, I'll save you!" Ash promised.

The Spearow formed a circle around Pikachu. Ash dove in to rescue his new Pokémon. Carrying Pikachu in his arms, Ash fled as fast as he could.

The path in the woods ended at the top of a big waterfall. And the Spearow were right behind them!

"Hold on tight!" Ash told Pikachu. Then he jumped.

Splash! The pair landed in the lake below. Ash tried to carry Pikachu back onto land, but they got caught in some fishing line.

A moment later, a redhead named Misty hoisted them out of the water. She was disappointed she hadn't caught a fish, but she was thrilled to see such a cute Pokémon!

Misty told Ash to take Pikachu to the Pokémon Center for a rest. (We'll get back to her on page 36. In the meantime, there's a Pikachu to save!)

Just then, Ash spotted Spearow in the sky. The

flock was even larger. There was no time to waste! Ash hopped on Misty's bike, put Pikachu in the front basket, and headed out to see Nurse Joy.

"Don't worry; I'll give it back someday!" Ash promised Misty as he pedaled away.

Storm clouds swept in, and the sky turned dark.

"Hang on, Pikachu, we're almost there," Ash said.

There was a clap of thunder, and rain began to fall. Worse yet, the flock of Spearow had tracked Ash and Pikachu down. They were nipping at Ash's ears.

"*Ack!*" Ash cried, pedaling as fast as he could. He didn't notice the small cliff ahead. The bike skidded off the edge and landed in a slippery mud patch. Ash and Pikachu were thrown off.

"Pikachu!" Ash cried.

"*Pika*," it whimpered.

Ash took out a Poké Ball and begged Pikachu to climb in to safety. But the stubborn Pokémon still didn't trust him. So Ash decided to try something rash to protect his new pal. He stood up and addressed the flock of angry Spearow.

"Spearow, I'm Ash Ketchum from Pallet Town. I'm destined to be the world's number-one Pokémon Master. So I can't be defeated by you! I'm going to capture all of you! Come and get me," Ash challenged them.

Pikachu was moved that Ash would put himself on the line like that. Now the Spearow had focused all their attention on Ash. Before they could attack, Pikachu leaped into the air and unleashed an incredible blast.

"*Piiiikachuuuuuuuuu!*" it screamed, shooting a huge bolt of electricity.

Pikachu's attack was so powerful that it scared away the Spearow AND cleared up the weather. The sun shone down on two new friends.

"We did it!" Ash cheered.

"*Pika.*" Pikachu nodded, exhausted.

Above, in the blue sky, a rare, Legendary Ho-Oh flew over a rainbow. Ash smiled. What a great end to his first day as a Pokémon Trainer!

The new bond between Ash and Pikachu would carry them through all kinds of trials as they traveled together. One thing was for sure—Ash and Pikachu were destined to be best friends forever.

PEOPLE IN THE POKÉMON WORLD

Ash is a Pokémon Trainer—someone who cares for Pokémon, trains with them, and battles for fun and for badges. But that's not the only pursuit for people who love Pokémon. Here are some of the other Pokémon-obsessed people Ash has met on his quest.

Dawn

POKÉMON COORDINATOR

Pokémon Coordinators train to compete in Pokémon Contests. Instead of using power and strategy, like in battles, contests are all about swagger and beauty. Coordinators work with their Pokémon to strut their stuff and get audiences oohing and aahing.

Ash's good friend Dawn is a decorated Pokémon Coordinator. To read more on her, head to page 88.

POKÉMON BREEDER

A Pokémon breeder is passionate about Pokémon health and well-being. They want their pals to feel good, look good, and be at their best overall. Breeders work hard to create healthy recipes for Poké food. They also keep their Pokémon well-groomed and make sure they get enough exercise to stay in peak athletic shape.

Although breeders are not focused on competing for trophies, their success is obvious when you see a well-cared-for Pokémon. One of Ash's closest friends, Brock, is a Pokémon breeder. Read more about him on page 30.

Brock

POKÉMON CONNOISSEUR

Partner, best friend, other half, team—these are all different ways of expressing one important thing. The relationship between Trainer and Pokémon is a delicate and important balance that really shows on the battlefield. A Pokémon Connoisseur is the person who can best tell if your team has what it takes to succeed.

To become a Connoisseur, you've got to study hard and pass tons of tests. It's that training that gives Connoisseurs the insights that make for great advice. So make sure the Connoisseur you visit has made the grade! They are ranked with an A, B, or C.

One of Ash's travel buddies and a Striaton City Gym Leader, Cilan, is a Rank A Connoisseur. Read more about him on page 115.

Cilan

Wattson

GYM LEADER

To compete in a League tournament, a Trainer must earn eight badges. The only way to do that is to challenge Gym Leaders around the region to a battle—and win!

Defeating these amazing Gym Leaders is no small task. They each have their own special strength. For example, jolly Wattson from Mauville City specializes in Electric-types and pranks (more on him on page 78). So watch your step, or you might just walk into one of his gags.

The Gym Leader of Azalea Town, Bugsy, specializes in Bug-types, like his name suggests. Lenora, of the Nacrene City Gym and Museum, is a Normal-type expert with more tricks up her sleeve than a magician.

Prof. Oak

POKÉMON PROFESSOR

Each region has a professor to guide new Trainers as they begin their journeys. The professors have very different personalities—from Professor Elm, Johto's shy bookworm, to Professor Birch, the outgoing hippie from Hoenn. And every professor has a different specialty, from Pokémon origins (Unova's Professor Juniper) to Pokémon habits and Evolution (Sinnoh's Professor Rowan).

But all professors have a few things in common: Each is in charge of a lab, each gives their region's new Trainers their first partner Pokémon, and each is named after a kind of tree!

POKÉMON PERFORMERS

Pokémon performers put on shows in special Pokémon Showcases. Aria, the Kalos Queen, presides over these events, so they're only found in her home region.

Ash and his pals first saw Aria and Braixen perform at a Pokémon Showcase in Lagoon Town. There are two sections of the Showcase—the Theme Performance and the Freestyle Performance. Each Pokémon has the chance to entertain an audience with its skill and beauty, plus they are free to use props.

Aria

POKÉMON CHAMPION

There is only one Trainer in each region who can call her- or himself Champion. They are the best of the best. Any Trainer can challenge a Champion to a battle, although it might be a challenge in and of itself to get one of them onto the battlefield! They are so wise and powerful that just chatting with one can inspire a Trainer to greatness.

Ash had the opportunity to befriend Cynthia, the Champion of Sinnoh (read more about her on page 102), and Alder, the Champion of Unova (read more about him on page 119).

Cynthia

NURSE JOY

One of a Pokémon Trainer's most important responsibilities is to keep their Pokémon healthy. So they have to take them for regular checkups at Pokémon Centers. Luckily, there are a lot of them spread across the Pokémon world. Every Pokémon Center looks different, but each one can be easily identified by the big "P" sign.

Pokémon Centers are run by sisters all named Nurse Joy. They've each made it their mission in life to provide excellent care for all Pokémon. They are very knowledgeable when it comes to healing tired, sick, and injured Pokémon. Nurse Joy relies on her attentive Pokémon Chansey, Blissey, Audino, or Comfey to help with her Pokémon patients.

NURSE JOYS' POKÉMON

AUDINO   BLISSEY   CHANSEY   COMFEY

OFFICER JENNY

Just like Nurse Joy, every Officer Jenny looks alike and talks alike. Perhaps that's because they're all related, too!

Every community is lucky to have a dutiful police officer named Jenny. If you spot an evildoer lurking around town, be sure to call on the best crime-stopper in the biz: Officer Jenny. Since there is strength in numbers, she always has a Pokémon pal by her side, and she often calls on Ash and his friends to help her catch the crooks.

SOME OF OFFICER JENNYS' POKÉMON

SPINARAK

GUMSHOOS   HERDIER   GROWLITHE

TEAM ROCKET

Since the moment Ash began his Pokémon journey, Jessie, James, and Meowth—members of the criminal organization Team Rocket—have been one step behind. They'll do just about anything to steal Pokémon, and they're particularly determined to get their hands on Ash's powerful Pikachu.

Team Rocket is a criminal organization bent on world domination. Fortunately for our heroes, they're not very good at it.

JESSIE

Jessie is the daughter of a famous Team Rocket operative. When she was very young, her mother left on assignment to track down the Mythical Pokémon Mew. So Jessie was raised mostly in a foster home. She grew up so poor that some of her meals were just snow.

Jessie's mother never returned from her mission, and Jessie had a hard time finding her way in the world without her mother's guidance. She tried nursing school and joining a bike gang. Eventually, she enrolled in Pokémon Tech—which is where she met James. Now Team Rocket is her whole world.

Jessie

JAMES

James comes from a very wealthy home—actually, make that more than one home. His family has mansions all over. James's parents are incredibly wealthy, but also incredibly strict. As a child, he was very lonely—his parents were too busy hosting fancy balls to pay him much attention. His only friend was Growlie, his loyal Growlithe.

When his parents made arrangements for him to marry a spoiled brat named Jessebelle, James fled from his life of luxury to find freedom. He enrolled in Pokémon Tech, where he met Jessie. They've been troublemaking together ever since.

James

MEOWTH

Meowth was abandoned as a baby. He wandered the streets, sad, alone, and hungry. Then one day he saw a Hollywood movie. Inspired by the food he saw onscreen, he decided to head to Hollywood himself.

But the city wasn't kind to him. Down on his luck, Meowth encountered a gang of other Meowth led by a Persian. They took him in and helped him find food.

One day, he spotted a beautiful Meowth named Meowsie. She told Meowth he didn't stand a chance with her because he wasn't human. So Meowth hid away in a local school and learned how to walk and talk like a human. He returned with flowers, but Meowsie just called him a freak. He didn't fit in anywhere—except for Team Rocket.

Meowth

BEWARE OF THESE VILLAINS

Jessie, James, and Meowth aren't the only villains Ash and Pikachu have to look out for. In fact, they're just a few of the goons in the larger Team Rocket organization. And Team Rocket isn't the only gang who's up to no good. There are many evil masterminds causing trouble all over the Pokémon world. Keep your eyes peeled for these bad guys and girls . . .

Giovanni

Butch & Cassidy

GIOVANNI

Jessie, James, and Meowth report to this Team Rocket manager. He always has his beloved Persian by his side. Although Giovanni is usually busy doling out orders, this big boss also hands out the Earth Badge as the Viridian City Gym Leader. His home base is in Kanto, but he likes to mess with every region.

DR. ZAGER

This mad scientist specializes in creating tech gadgets for Team Rocket.

BUTCH AND CASSIDY

Beware, this Team Rocket duo is up to no good in Kanto, Johto, Hoenn, and Sinnoh.

TEAM PLASMA

If you're in Unova, look out for this evil organization. Ghetsis, Colress, Aldith, Schwarz, and Weiss are tirelessly plotting a takeover of Unova—and of Reshiram.

HUNTER J

This Sinnoh-based Pokémon poacher will stop at nothing to steal Pokémon she can sell on the black market.

Hunter J

TEAM GALACTIC

This team might take its names from the planets—Saturn, Jupiter, and Mars—but they think they're the center of the universe. Under Commander Cyrus, they're after valuable Sinnoh artifacts and Legendary Pokémon Azelf, Uxie, and Mesprit.

TEAM MAGMA

Lead by Maxie, Team Magma has a special interest in making more ground for them to control in Hoenn. As their name suggests, they're focused on capturing the Legendary Pokémon of magma, Groudon, and the Red Orb that controls it.

Team Galactic

TEAM AQUA

Team Magma is all about land, and their rivals, Team Aqua, are all about the ocean. Led by Archie, goons like Shelly and Brodie work hard to capture the Legendary Pokémon Kyogre and the Blue Orb that controls it.

TEAM SKULL

In the Alola region, a group of bullies known as Team Skull are bad to the bone. Tupp, Zipp, and Rapp are a terrible trio who have made it their mission to cause a lot of trouble. They like to talk tough, pick fights, and steal other people's Pokémon.

Team Skull

KANTO

This colorful region is Ash's home—he comes from Pallet Town, to be exact. Every city besides his hometown is named after a special color: Lavender Town, Saffron City, Cinnabar Island, and so on. And if you're into battles or the color blue, there's also the Indigo Conference.

It's no wonder that a region with cities named after every color of the rainbow boasts a beautiful view—especially if you're traveling on the famous bridge to Vermilion City.

Ready to check it out? Go to the next page to explore Kanto with Ash!

PALLET TOWN

Both Ash and his mentor, Professor Oak, call Pallet Town home. It's a sleepy town nestled in the foothills of a mountain range near a river—the perfect pastoral spot for a travel-weary Trainer to rest and recharge.

ASH'S MOM

Ash's mom, Delia, is his biggest cheerleader and also his fashion stylist. She's so handy! Not only is she great at sewing Ash's clothing, she also tends a beautiful garden in the backyard.

Mr. Mime keeps Delia company and helps her around the house when Ash is traveling. She's very proud of Ash's good sportsmanship and the care he takes of his friends, both human and Pokémon. Whether he wins or loses, Ash's mom just loves how he's playing the game.

MR. MIME

When this Pokémon showed up on Delia's doorstep, she thought it was Ash dressed up in a costume! Mr. Mime and Delia became fast friends, and she has really grown to depend on her affectionately nicknamed "Mimey." Ever since Mimey helped stop a surprise visit from Team Rocket, it and Delia have been inseparable.

PROFESSOR OAK

Professor Samuel Oak is one of the most important Pokémon researchers, but he is best known as the inventor of the Pokédex. His lab in Pallet Town is easy to spot because it sits atop a hill marked by a big windmill.

Professor Oak's lab is just up the road from the house where Ash grew up. But no matter how far Ash travels, he stays close to the professor. When Ash needs some words of wisdom, he calls his pal Professor Oak. Not only is he full of good advice, he can also say it in a rhyme. (He's known for his poetry.)

Professor Oak gave Ash his first Pokémon ever—and his best friend—Pikachu! When Ash travels to new regions, he leaves his Pokémon friends to play with his favorite professor.

KANTO FIRST PARTNER POKÉMON

BULBASAUR

This Grass-type Pokémon is a sun-loving, fun-loving friend! It wants nothing more than to soak up some rays while it naps. Sunbathing is super-relaxing—plus, it makes the seed on Bulbasaur's back grow.

BULBASAUR EVOLVES INTO IVYSAUR, THEN VENUSAUR.

SQUIRTLE

The Tiny Turtle Pokémon is one speedy swimmer, thanks to the grooves in its shell. A special group of this Water-type Pokémon also learned that they make awesome firefighters—more on that on the next page!

SQUIRTLE EVOLVES INTO WARTORTLE, THEN BLASTOISE.

CHARMANDER

You can tell a lot about this Fire-type Pokémon by the torch tip of its tail. When it's happy, the flame dances. When it's ready to battle, the flame burns big and bright.

CHARMANDER EVOLVES INTO CHARMELEON, THEN CHARIZARD.

SQUIRTLE

Ash's travel pal Squirtle was the leader of a cool group of Pokémon called the Squirtle Squad. They all wear shades, and they're all brave. Sadly, they were also all abandoned by their Trainers. But they turned those tough times around by banding together.

When Team Rocket tried to trick the Squirtle Squad into stealing Ash's Pikachu, the Water-type Pokémon realized they make great firefighters. Now they help Officer Jenny put out blazes in Kanto.

CHARMANDER

Ash first met his friend Charmander while traveling through the woods. It refused to move from the spot where its Trainer had left it, because it was sure he'd come back. So it waited and waited—even through a bad storm, which made it sick.

Ash rescued Charmander and brought it to the Pokémon Center. There, it realized it had found the friend it needed in Ash, and it joined him on his journey.

Charmander was still the same willful Pokémon. It often refused to listen to Ash, but it grew strong enough to evolve into Charmeleon after helping end an Exeggutor rampage. Later on, during a battle with Aerodactyl, it evolved into Charizard. As this Pokémon grew bigger and stronger, so did its pride.

BULBASAUR

Ash was lucky enough to catch Bulbasaur by battling it against his Pikachu. Their friendship may have started with a fight, but Bulbasaur proved itself to be a wonderful peacemaker. It is so renowned for its goodwill that Professor Oak called Bulbasaur back to the lab to mediate between Pokémon who wouldn't stop arguing.

KRABBY

Ash caught Krabby while showing off for Misty. Since he was already traveling with six Pokémon, he sent it to live at Professor Oak's lab. During their short time together, Ash was able to help Krabby evolve into Kingler.

MUK

The only thing stronger than Muk's moves is its stench. While it has its opponents saying *pee-yew*, it does have a nose for a good battle. And with Ash as its Trainer, its skills definitely don't stink.

TAUROS

Ash caught Tauros during his travels through a special part of the Kanto region known as the Safari Zone. Tauros and Ash battled together during the final round of the Orange League.

SNORLAX

This hungry Pokémon has an appetite for battle. It can destroy a garden—and its opponents—in no time flat. In fact, that's how Ash first met Snorlax. The locals in the Orange Islands were worried it would chow down on all their fruit. So Ash wisely asked Jigglypuff to sing Snorlax to sleep.

Once Snorlax was snoozing, Ash and Pikachu were able to catch the incredible eater. But Ash can rarely take Snorlax on his adventures, because he can never fit enough food for it into his backpack.

PIDGEOTTO

The first Pokémon Ash tried to catch was Pidgey. He was too inexperienced, but as the saying goes, "If at first you don't succeed, try, try again!" With a little bit of practice and strategy, Ash and Pikachu were able to catch its evolved form, Pidgeotto.

First, Ash tried catching the Normal-Flying-type with Caterpie. When that didn't work, Pikachu stepped in with Thundershock to seal the deal. During their travels, Pidgeotto evolved into Pidgeot while protecting some Pidgey from a Fearow attack.

CATERPIE

The first Pokémon Ash ever caught is Caterpie—in a very unusual way. There was no battle, no back and forth, no bonding. Ash simply tossed his Poké Ball at the Bug-type and caught it.

This green guy completely freaked out Misty, Ash's travel partner. She said it must be a weakling to have gotten caught so easily. But Caterpie proved itself a valuable member of Ash's team when it stopped Team Rocket in their tracks by wrapping them in String Shot.

BROCK

The former Gym Leader of Pewter City, Brock is a Rock-type expert. That might explain why he sometimes appears stone-faced. But beneath that cool exterior, he is actually a really sensitive guy.

Brock is a caretaker by nature. He is always happy to cook for his friends. Both Pokémon and people line up when they hear Brock is whipping up something to eat! So it's no wonder he's destined to become one of the best Pokémon breeders.

To follow his dreams, Brock left behind his big family and joined Ash on his journey. (For the full story on how they became buds, just turn the page.) They've been travel pals through four regions: Kanto, Johto, Hoenn, and Sinnoh. Even when Ash and Brock have gone their separate ways, they always end up crossing paths again, and they're always happy to be reunited!

Brock is crazy about Pokémon, but he's even more girl-crazy. The would-be charmer will chase any lady. Although he thinks his tactics are impressive, he is often met with a harsh reality—rejection. But Brock remains confident. On rare occasions, his dramatic flair even works! And sometimes, it helps separate the good guys from the bad guys. Not only can Brock tell identical relatives like Officer Jenny and Nurse Joy apart, he can also tell if they're imposters! Look out, Jessie—no matter how good your disguise is, it won't fool Brock.

BROCK'S POKÉMON

Brock specializes in caring for Pokémon. So his pals know that Brock always has their back.

KANTO

GEODUDE

ONIX ⇨ STEELIX

ZUBAT ⇨ GOLBAT ⇨ CROBAT

JOHTO

PINECO ⇨ FORRETRESS

HOENN

MUDKIP ⇨ MARSHTOMP

LOTAD ⇨ LOMBRE ⇨ LUDICOLO

SINNOH

BONSLY ⇨ SUDOWOODO

HAPPINY

CROAGUNK

HOW BROCK AND ASH BECAME BUDS

Ash and Misty were making their way through the Viridian Forest when Ash spotted his next challenge.

"There it is!" Ash exclaimed. "I can't wait to earn my first badge at the Pewter City Gym!"

"*Pika pika!*" Pikachu cheered.

Ash, Pikachu, and Misty hurried down to the city. On their way, they stumbled on a big rock and an even bigger personality.

"The name's Flint," said a rough-looking guy in a red knit cap. "Want to buy a precious Pewter City rock from my shop?"

"Uh, I'm actually looking to collect Gym badges, not rocks," Ash explained.

"Want me to show you the way to Brock's?" Flint offered.

"Yes, take me to this 'Brock's' Gym. I'll beat him!" Ash declared.

"You'll beat him, huh?" Flint laughed. "He's one of the best!"

"I'd be happy to help you practice for the big battle," Misty offered.

"I don't need help. I'm going to win my first badge myself!" Ash replied.

As Ash stepped inside the Gym, a spotlight lit up a boy with spiky hair seated atop a stone staircase. It was the famous Gym Leader Brock.

When Ash challenged Brock to a battle, it was obvious this was Ash's first Gym battle. Ash was a little embarrassed, but grateful when Brock explained the League rules. Each Trainer must battle with two Pokémon each.

"Are you planning on battling with Pikachu?" Brock asked.

Ash nodded.

"It can't win; it's too cute!" Brock warned.

"You worry about your Pokémon, and I'll worry about mine," Ash snapped back.

But the minute the battle began, it was clear Ash was in over his head. When Brock chose a giant Onix as his first Pokémon, Pikachu ran off the battlefield and hid under Ash's shirt. Ash gave Pikachu a pep talk to get it ready to rock that Rock-type.

Onix led off with Tackle, and Pikachu tried to flee again. Except this time, Onix wrapped its long tail around the little Electric-type.

"Pikachu, use Thunderbolt to get out of its grip!" Ash suggested.

But Pikachu's Thunderbolt wasn't strong enough to rattle Onix. So Ash tried to have Pikachu return, but it couldn't— it was trapped!

"Do you surrender?" Brock asked.

For the sake of his best friend, Ash retreated. Defeated and deflated, he took Pikachu to the Pokémon Center to rest. On the way, he and Misty ran into Flint, who offered them a place to recharge.

As Pikachu napped, Flint reassured Ash that losing a match is something that happens to everyone who battles. "It's hard work getting in shape for matches," Flint said.

When Pikachu woke up, they all headed out for an evening walk. As they strolled through town, Ash wondered why a talented guy like Brock had never been in a regional championship. Flint explained that Brock had never even left Pewter City.

"Brock isn't just a terrific Gym Leader and Trainer, he's also one incredible older brother," Flint explained. "Brock's dad ran out on his family to become a Pokémon Trainer, and no one's heard from him since. Brock is all his little brothers and sisters have left. He cooks, cleans, and cares for all ten of them."

"Whoa, what an amazing guy!" Ash replied.

Flint led Ash and Pikachu down to the town's old water mill—a shack with a big wooden wheel sitting atop a dried-up riverbed.

"This old hydroelectric plant will help supercharge Pikachu," Flint promised.

"Really?" Ash asked. "That's awesome!"

"Well, the only problem is there's no river water to make it work. So you'll have to run in the wheel yourself," Flint added.

It was enough to help Ash get back his fighting spirit. He ran and ran until

Pikachu was so powered up, the little Electric-type lit up the shack with its energy.

The next morning, Ash and Pikachu returned to the rock-solid Pewter City Gym to challenge Brock.

"Geodude, I choose you!" Brock began.

"Pidgeotto, start with Gust!" Ash responded.

Pidgeotto fanned Geodude with its wings, but it didn't work. Brock explained that Flying-types are weak against Rock-types. Geodude barely had to make a move, and Pidgeotto was too tired to keep battling.

To make matters worse, all ten of Brock's little brothers and sisters came to watch the match. So did Misty.

Ash chose his pal Pikachu as his second and last Pokémon. It took to the field, ready for battle.

"*Piiiikachuuuuuuuuuu!*" it screamed, unleashing a huge electric explosion. Geodude was cooked. Its gray stone was completely covered in black soot. Brock asked Geodude to return, and then he called on Onix.

"*Pikachuuuuu!*" Ash's Pokémon yelped.

Pikachu was all powered up, but its attacks weren't focused. It shot electricity all over the Gym, missing Onix. But it did start an electrical fire.

"Okay, Onix, use Bind!" Brock called. Pikachu was all wrapped up in the giant Rock Snake Pokémon's tail!

"*Piiiiika!*" it shouted, trying to wriggle out of Onix's grip.

Suddenly, the emergency sprinkler system went off, showering water onto the battlefield.

"Rock-type Pokémon are weakened by water," Misty called from the stands. "Now's your chance!"

Ash was about to go for the easy win, but his conscience stopped him. Ash thought about what a strong role model Brock was to his siblings. He didn't want to take a cheap shot and beat Brock in front of them.

Before Ash could decide what to do, Brock's siblings crawled all over him.

"You're a big bully!" one brother shouted.

"You leave my brother alone!" a sister yelled.

"Enough, you guys. This is an official match!" Brock shouted.

But Ash didn't want to keep fighting. In their last match, when Pikachu was weak, Brock had stopped battling. Ash wanted to show him the same respect.

"Winning the match like this doesn't prove anything," Ash told Brock. "Next time we battle, I'll win fair and square."

Ash thanked Brock and left the Gym with Pikachu by his side.

"Thank you, Pikachu," Ash said. "I'm sorry if the training was a little hard on you, but you were so great in there!"

Suddenly, Ash heard his name called. It was Brock!

"You deserve this," Brock said, handing Ash the Boulder Badge. "You know, I never really cared about battles. I've always wanted to become the world's best Pokémon breeder. But I can't leave my family. So I'm counting on you to take this badge and fulfill your dreams for me!"

"Thank you," Ash replied, honored. "I'll do my best to prove I'm worthy of the Boulder Badge."

Suddenly, Flint emerged from the woods nearby. He ripped off his fake beard and revealed his true identity.

"Dad!" Brock cried.

Flint explained that he'd turned out to be a terrible Trainer, but he'd been too embarrassed to return to his family a failure—until Ash had inspired him to return home and take care of his children.

"Now it's your turn to follow your heart," Flint told Brock.

With that, Brock was free to begin his journey. And the perfect travel buddy was standing right next to him.

"Can I come along with you, Ash?" Brock asked.

"Of course," Ash replied. "It'll be good to travel with an awesome guy like you!"

MISTY

The Cerulean City Gym Leaders—Daisy, Violet, and Lily—are better known as the "Three Sensational Sisters," a beautiful synchronized swimming team. But there is also a fourth little sister and Gym Leader, Misty, who's always been the odd one out. She has a lot to prove, and she sets out on her journey determined to show her sisters just how fabulous the girl they call a "runt" really is!

While fishing in a river outside of Pallet Town, Misty accidentally caught Ash and Pikachu. She couldn't get over just how cute the little yellow Pokémon was—until it accidentally zapped her bike to bits with a terrific Thunder Shock.

At first, Misty followed Ash and Pikachu around because she was determined to get them to replace her bike. But eventually, she stopped hassling Ash for new wheels and just came along for the ride.

Ash, Misty, and Brock traveled and trained together through Johto and Kanto. When Misty finally returned home to the Cerulean City Gym, her hard work finally paid off. She went on to enjoy her new reputation as the best Gym Leader in town.

MISTY'S POKÉMON

One of the keepers of the Cascade Badge, Misty loves Water-types.

KANTO

STARYU ⇨ STARMIE   GOLDEEN

HORSEA   PSYDUCK   LUVDISC

JOHTO

POLIWAG ⇨ POLIWHIRL ⇨ POLITOED

TOGEPI ⇨ TOGETIC   CORSOLA   AZURILL

GARY OAK

Ash's biggest rival grew up with him in Pallet Town. Both Trainers got their first partner Pokémon on the same day, but Ash and Gary couldn't be more different.

When Gary began his journey, he was so cocky that he traveled around with a group of cheerleaders to root him on. Gary is the grandson of Ash's mentor, Professor Oak, but it seemed like this apple had fallen pretty far from the tree. Gary felt like he had to be the best to live up to his name, so he was eager to tell everyone else they weren't as good as him.

Although Gary was an incredible Trainer in battle, the challenges he faced on his journey humbled him. After Ash battled him at the Johto Silver Conference (get the full story on page 52!), Gary decided to follow in Professor Oak's footsteps and become a Pokémon researcher.

The next time Ash ran into Gary, he was pleasantly surprised to find out that his rival had turned into a cool dude who'd really found his calling. Gary now assists Professor Rowan with his research in Sinnoh.

BLASTOISE

NIDOQUEEN

NIDOKING

SCIZOR

ARCANINE

DODUO

DODRIO

EEVEE

UMBREON

MAGMAR

GOLEM

ELECTIVIRE

THE BATTLE FOR THE EARTH BADGE

Ash needed one more badge to enter the Pokémon League, and it would turn out to be his toughest battle yet. He already knew the man he'd have to challenge, the Viridian City Gym Leader, Giovanni, because he was also a Team Rocket boss. Giovanni was also infamous for having a secret, powerful Pokémon he'd used to defeat Gary Oak.

But Ash was determined. He strode into the Gym ready to battle! And Giovanni was a no-show. He'd gone off on assignment and left his Gym in the care of Jessie, James, and Meowth.

As you might expect, it didn't turn out to be a fair fight. The arena was covered with traps that shocked, zapped, and boomed. All those booby traps combined to make this Ash's trickiest battle yet.

Then suddenly—and amazingly—Gary stepped in and put a stop to all that Team Rocket nonsense. But Jessie, James, and Meowth still wouldn't play fair and square. Without her bag of tricks, Jessie panicked and changed the battle rules, allowing more Pokémon into the battle.

But the joke was on her when Pikachu took the field and blew the competition away with a shocking win. And so Ash earned his Earth Badge—and his spot in the Pokémon League Championship.

THE RAINBOW BADGE

Ash has a nose for battle, but not for perfume. The sweet scent of flowers and fruits are wasted on him. It's an opinion he proudly stated in the famed perfume shop in Celadon City.

Little did Ash know that behind all those bottles lay the Celadon City Gym. Erika wasn't just the Gym Leader, she was also the owner of the perfume shop that Ash insulted. It was a secret smell test, and Ash had just failed.

But Ash isn't the kind of guy who's willing to give up, even if it meant having to disguise himself as a girl. Erika wouldn't battle Ash, but perhaps she'd battle "Ashley." With the help of costume experts Team Rocket, he dressed up in a blonde wig and challenged Erika to a Gym battle.

Just when it looked like Ash's ruse had worked, Pikachu's Thunderbolt zapped away his wig and revealed his true identity. Worse yet, while Erika was distracted by the battle, Jessie, James, and Meowth stole her secret perfume formula—and managed to escape by starting a fire.

In a flash, everyone evacuated the Gym. Ash and Misty teamed up with their Water-type Pokémon, Squirtle and Staryu, to fight the blaze. Meanwhile, Erika was growing frantic because she couldn't find her Gloom. Ash dashed into the Gym to rescue the scared Pokémon. Erika was so grateful for Ash's help, she awarded him the Rainbow Badge.

ASH'S FIRST REGIONAL CHAMPIONSHIP— THE INDIGO LEAGUE

After earning eight Gym badges in the Kanto region, Ash qualified for the Indigo League—and so did his rival, Gary Oak. Although Gary went on TV to trash-talk Ash, Ash was determined not to get psyched out.

He started his first round by taking Professor Oak's advice and switching up his Pokémon. His bold choice, Krabby, paid off, and during the battle it evolved into Kingler. Ash won the match against Mandy.

Ash won his second battle on a rock field with ease, but in the third battle he was on thin ice—literally. The battlefield was frozen water, and Ash's opponent, Pete, and his Arcanine pinned Pikachu in a corner. Then Ash called on the Electric-type to use its tough Thunderbolt, and it won the match in one big zap.

Gary was eliminated from the competition in the fourth round—before Ash. It was a tough blow, but his ego was too big to let him admit he was upset.

Ash's fourth round was a heated battle with Jeanette. Her Bellsprout, Beedrill, and Scyther put up quite a fight. Although Bulbasaur and Pikachu tried their hardest to nab a victory, Ash won at the last minute with his surprising third-choice Pokémon—Muk.

Before Ash could battle Richie in the next round, the two had to fend off Team Rocket. Defeating the bad guys really bonded Ash and Richie, but the round had to go on. On the battlefield, Richie proved his reputation for being a tough opponent. After forging a friendship, Charizard was reluctant to battle Sparky, Richie's Pikachu. So Ash forfeited the match to his new pal. He might not have won his first League Championship, but he made it far and made new friends, too!

LEGENDARY POKÉMON OF KANTO

MEWTWO

Scientists created this Pokémon by manipulating Mew's genes. Mewtwo is incredibly powerful, but its heart is savage.

ARTICUNO

This Pokémon has the power of ice. As it flies, snow falls with each flap of its wings.

MOLTRES

This Pokémon is so hot, the heat waves it emits make it nearly impossible to spot.

ZAPDOS

Known for its electric power, Zapdos recharges itself in lightning storms.

MYTHICAL POKÉMON OF KANTO

MEW

Some believe that Mew's cells hold the genetic code for every Pokémon. This Mythical Pokémon can turn invisible to keep others from noticing it.

JOHTO

Johto is a hop, skip, and a jump from Kanto. A quick boat ride from Olivine City or a speed-train trip from Saffron City will get Trainers there in no time.

If you love hiking, you won't be disappointed by a visit to Johto. This region is known for the sprawling green forest that covers it. And Johto isn't just green in color, it also has a reputation for being eco-friendly. No matter where you land in Johto, you're never far from the peace and quiet of nature.

Johto also boasts one of the biggest urban jungles—Goldenrod City. There are so many interesting spots in different corners of the city that it's easy to get lost or happen upon a dead-end street. To travelers and even locals, Goldenrod can seem more like a maze than a city.

JOHTO FIRST PARTNER POKÉMON

TOTODILE

The Big Jaw Pokémon is always yapping, but its loud bark isn't half as bad as its powerful bite. Totodile might be small, but those chompers are a huge advantage on the battlefield.

TOTODILE EVOLVES INTO CROCONAW, THEN FERALIGATR.

CHIKORITA

The cute leaf on Chikorita's head is more than just decoration—it provides a sound battle strategy. Chikorita can woo even the angriest opponent with the sweet scent of its leaf.

CHIKORITA EVOLVES INTO BAYLEEF, THEN MEGANIUM.

CYNDAQUIL

Cyndaquil is on fire—truly! The Fire Mouse's back is covered in a blaze that burns brightly when it's ready to battle. If it's too tired, the flames fizzle like a stove that won't light.

CYNDAQUIL EVOLVES INTO QUILAVA, THEN TYPHLOSION.

PROFESSOR ELM

Once you get Professor Elm talking about his research, there's no stopping him. Elm helms the New Bark Town lab, a place where many researchers conduct their studies. Professor Elm is also the renowned author of *A Brilliant Analysis of the Hypersized Communicative Faculties of Pokémon*, and the head of the Pokémon Preservation Council. So it's no wonder he's a close friend of Professor Oak. In fact, he and Oak like to debate Pokémon research findings on a regular basis.

Professor Elm might come off as nerdy, but if studying Pokémon too hard is wrong, he doesn't want to be right. And Ash is happy to help him with his research. He even brings Professor Elm back an Egg from the Pokémon Marine Conservatory, and it hatches into Larvitar.

CYNDAQUIL

While wandering the forest, Ash happened upon a spot particularly known for Cyndaquil. Team Rocket had heard the same rumor. Before Ash could try to catch one, Team Rocket, in a ridiculous robot, stepped in to steal it. Ash rescued Cyndaquil from their grip himself. When it still wasn't safe, he threw a Poké Ball and got the Fire-type out of the fray. Ash and Cyndaquil have been buddies ever since.

CHIKORITA

Following their sweet smell, Ash sniffed out a group of Chikorita sitting in the sun. He decided to catch one . . . and in doing so landed both Charizard and Chikorita in the Pokémon Center.

Nurse Joy told Ash that the Chikorita in the area are particularly stubborn. Before long, Team Rocket caught wind of the aromatic Chikorita and decided to try to steal it. Chikorita escaped, but Ash found it freezing in the snow. When Ash risked himself to rescue the Grass-type Pokémon, he caught a new friend.

HERACROSS

Ash came across Heracross in a part of the woods where all the trees had mysteriously died. Ash was determined to save the Pokémon habitat, and at first he thought the wild, hungry Heracross were to blame for the damage. But he soon realized it was Team Rocket at the heart of the trouble. After battling the bad guys together, Ash realized he'd made a good friend in one particular Heracross, and it joined Ash on his journey.

NOCTOWL

When Ash threw his Poké Ball at a wild Noctowl, it threw it right back at him. However, Ash wasn't the only one who wanted to catch this intelligent Pokémon. Team Rocket got up to their usual tricks, so Ash and his friends Bulbasaur and Chikorita Vine Whipped them away. Noctowl was so impressed that it challenged Ash to a battle. When he won, he caught his new Normal-Flying-type friend.

TOTODILE

While fishing for a Water-type Pokémon, Ash and Misty spotted a wild Totodile and tossed their Poké Balls at it at the exact same time. Since no one was sure who actually caught it, they decided to resolve the matter with a three-on-three battle! During the fight, Misty's Poliwag evolved into Poliwhirl, but it was Bulbasaur's Solar Beam that won the match.

Totodile and Ash became a great team immediately. And Totodile quickly proved its loyalty and strength by helping Ash blast off Team Rocket.

PHANPY

Ash didn't catch this Pokémon—he hatched it from an Egg he won. As Phanpy grew, so did their friendship.

ASH vs. GARY: SHOWDOWN!

Ash and Gary are the same age, from the same town, and started out on their journey as Trainers at the same time from the same lab. So you'd think they'd be best friends—but instead they became sworn rivals.

It all started when their fishing lines got crossed at a lake near Pallet Town, before their Pokémon journeys began. Ash was hoping to catch a Water-type, but he couldn't even snare a Magikarp.

"Let me show you how it's done," Gary bragged.

But when they both felt something tugging on their lines, it wound up being the same thing—a Poké Ball. The treasure snapped in two as they pulled it out, and each boy got half. Ash and Gary each kept their half as a symbol of commitment to training—and as a reminder of their rivalry.

As the two traveled through Kanto and Johto, their paths kept crossing. The two Trainers ultimately met at the Johto Silver Conference. It was the biggest tournament either Trainer had ever competed in—and a chance for them to settle the score. The quarterfinal round pitted Ash against Gary in a six-on-six Pokémon battle.

"Ash, your Silver Conference experience is going to be a short one," Gary declared. "I hope you had fun."

"There's no way I'm losing to you, Gary!" Ash replied.

That night, Ash stayed up for hours, researching Gary and his Pokémon. His rival didn't seem to favor any Pokémon type—it was impossible to guess whom he'd use.

Luckily, Ash got some help with his decision in the form of a surprise flying high in the sky.

"*Charizard!*" his Fire-Flying-type said, swooping down to greet Ash.

"Am I glad to see you!" Ash cheered. "How'd you know I needed you, buddy?"

"I made a phone call last night," Brock admitted.

What's more, Professor Oak and Delia, Ash's mom, had arrived to cheer him on. As for Gary, he brought his own professional cheerleading team.

The next day, Ash stepped onto the field ready to fight! The battlefield was covered in boulders. Gary chose his powerful Drill Pokémon, Nidoqueen. Ash called on his terrific Normal-type Pokémon, Tauros.

"Let the match begin!" the judge shouted.

Nidoqueen kicked things off with Rock Smash, making it rain stones onto the battlefield. Ash tried to have Tauros knock the rocks away, but it was no use.

"We'll have to go with a straightforward attack. Tauros, use Horn Attack!" Ash commanded.

Tauros raced over with incredible force, head down, horns out. *"Taaaurooooooooooos!"* it shouted.

But Gary told Nidoqueen to grab it by the horns. The mighty Tauros was stopped in its tracks!

Gary seized the moment to have Nidoqueen use its fierce Hyper Beam.

"Niiiidoqueen!" it yelped, firing a big ray of light at Tauros.

"Oh, no, Tauros!" Ash cried. "Return."

With one bold attack, Tauros was knocked out of the competition.

"You may have battled all the rest, but our man, Gary, is the best!" Gary's cheerleaders sang.

Everyone in the arena was wondering whom Ash would battle with next.

"Heracross, I choose you!" Ash cried, throwing his next Poké Ball.

"Heracross!" it cried, ready to battle.

Smart at strategy, Gary decided to substitute

Magmar for Nidoqueen because a Fire-type would have the advantage. Magmar started the round by shooting a blazing Flamethrower, but Heracross swiftly dodged it.

"Hera heracross!" It struck Magmar with Fury Swipes.

Gary decided to heat up the battle with a Fire Pokémon's most powerful attack: Fire Blast.

"Maaaagmaaaaar!" his Pokémon screamed.

"Now add Flamethrower!" Gary instructed.

Before Heracross took the hit, Ash suggested, "Flap your wings to blow the flames away, Heracross!"

Using its wings, Heracross created a gust of wind so strong, it blew out the fire.

"Way to go, Heracross," Ash cheered. "Now use Megahorn!"

Magmar tried to hit Heracross with Flamethrower, but Megahorn was already glowing with incredible power. It earned a direct hit for Heracross!

"Magmar is unable to battle," the judge announced. "Heracross wins!"

"You see, Gary, my Pokémon are powerful enough to win without type advantage!" Ash bragged.

The match was tied—one to one!

"I guess it's time to show him my best! Deal with this, Ashy-boy," Gary cried, pulling out his strongest Pokémon.

"Blastoise, I choose you!"

"Blastoise!" the big Pokémon boomed.

Heracross struck first with Fury Swipes. Blastoise's response was a shocking hit of Hydro Pump—the strongest Ash had ever seen.

"Blastoooiiise!" it cried, spraying a sharp stream of water.

"Shield yourself with the rocks!" Ash called to Heracross.

But Blastoise's Hydro Pump was so

powerful, it blew the rocks away. There was nowhere to hide. Blastoise won the round!

"Gary, Gary, number one! Show the losers how it's done!" Gary's cheerleaders sang.

Ash was under pressure to make the perfect next pick. "Muk, I choose you!" he said, tossing his Poké Ball.

His choice surprised the crowd, but Ash was a man with a plan.

"Blastoooise!" Gary's Pokémon shouted, charging to headbutt Muk with Skull Bash.

"Show that Blastoise! Use Sludge Bomb!" Ash instructed Muk.

"Muk muk muk!" it screamed, firing dirt balls at Blastoise.

Blastoise hit the dirt balls as if they were baseballs. It slipped into its shell and used Rapid Spin. Then it spun right into Muk!

"Quick, Muk, surround it!" Ash called.

Muk covered Blastoise with its sludgy body. Now Blastoise was stuck in its shell—and stuck in Muk!

"Blastoise!" it yelped, blasting its way out with Hydro Pump.

"Quick, Muk, return!" Ash instructed. "Bayleef, I choose you!"

Ash's fourth Pokémon stepped onto the battlefield.

"Bayleef!" Ash's Pokémon shouted, ready for action.

Blastoise started the battle with Hydro Pump, but Ash was expecting that.

"Bayleef, use Vine Whip to jump up!" Ash shouted.

"Bayleeeeeeeef!" it cheered as it leaped high above the battlefield.

From the sky, Bayleef shot Razor Leaf. Blastoise returned to its shell and deflected the leaf hits with Rapid Spin. So Bayleef put all its weight into landing on Blastoise with Body Slam.

When Bayleef got close, Blastoise used Bite to catch it by the green leaf on its head. Then Blastoise spun Bayleef around and around.

"Bay bay bay bayleef!" it cried as it swirled through the air.

"Bayleef, you were great! You deserve a long rest," Ash whispered to his pal as he called it back.

It was time for Ash's fifth Pokémon of the match. "Gary and his Pokémon are very impressive, but so are we!" Ash rallied his troops. "I choose you, Snorlax!"

Once he saw Ash's pick, Gary decided to switch out Blastoise. The next round would be Ash and Snorlax versus Gary and Arcanine.

"Snorlaaaax!" the roly-poly Pokémon said.

Gary told Arcanine to start with Take Down. Ash asked Snorlax to beat

Arcanine to the punch with Body Slam.

"Arcanine, dodge it and use Fire Spin!" Gary shouted.

Arcanine's fiery blast froze Snorlax in flames.

"Don't give up, Snorlax!" Ash cheered. "Hit it with Hyper Beam!"

"*Snooooorrrlaaaaax!*" it shouted, shooting a steady stream of light.

With that one direct hit, Arcanine was no longer able to battle. The match went to Snorlax and Ash!

Gary brought Nidoqueen back out. Then he stole a play out of Ash's book. He had Nidoqueen jump up high to deliver Double Kick. But Snorlax dodged it and threw an Ice Punch so powerful that Nidoqueen was knocked out!

"How'd Snorlax get so fast?" Gary wondered.

Scizor, Gary's next Pokémon pick, landed on the battlefield. Its speed gave it a total advantage against Snorlax. It was able to hit Snorlax with super-fast Quick Attacks, a blast of Hyper Beam, and a swipe of Metal Claw before the Sleeping Pokémon could even make a move.

Snorlax was unable to battle, and Scizor won the round. So Ash called on Muk again.

"*Scizor!*" Gary's Pokémon howled.

But Muk gave Scizor a push right back. Gary had Scizor grab on to Muk with Metal Claw, then throw it in the air.

"Now, use Swift!" Gary told Scizor.

Sharp, shiny stars flew at Muk, knocking it out. Scizor had won another round.

Ash had to pick his final Pokémon. "It's time!" he cried as he tossed his last Poké Ball. "Let's go, Charizard!"

"*Charizard!*" it called.

All it took was one fierce blast of Flamethrower, and Charizard won the round against Scizor.

Gary chose his sixth and final Pokémon: Golem. Gary and his Rock-Ground-type had the type advantage over Ash and his Fire-Flying-type.

"*Golem!*" it shouted, sending a Magnitude shock wave to start the battle.

"Carry it into the sky, Charizard," Ash instructed.

But that was easier said than done—Golem was more than twice as heavy as

Charizard! Charizard used all its strength to lift Golem. It tried to land Seismic Toss, but it couldn't.

"We'll get it next time, Charizard!" Ash cheered.

Gary didn't waste a moment in this tense final round. "Use Rollout, now!" he shouted.

"Charizard, Dragon Rage!" Ash cried.

"Charizaaarrrrrd!" it screamed, shooting a fireball right into Golem.

"Goooolem," it sighed, unable to battle.

Now Ash and Gary were both down to their very last Pokémon—the heat was on!

"You've gotten this far, Ashy-boy," Gary mocked. "And that'll be as far as you get!"

The final round was Charizard versus Blastoise. Again, Gary had the type advantage. Ash knew he had to strike first and strike hard.

"Charizard, Flamethrower!" Ash called.

Charizard shot fire straight at Blastoise, but Gary had it twirl with Rapid Spin to deflect the blaze.

"Blastooooise!" it shouted, surprising Charizard with Hydro Pump.

Ash had Charizard fly out of the watery fray, but Blastoise headbutted it with Skull Bash. Charizard took to the air and managed to escape Blastoise's next move.

Charizard was doing a great job dodging attacks, but playing defense was no way to win. Ash had to come up with a strategy. "Come on, there's got to be something I can do," he muttered nervously.

Then a light bulb went off in his head. "That's it!" Ash proclaimed. "Charizard, use Flamethrower to burn the battlefield!"

No one could figure out Ash's plan, not even Gary. Until—slowly—the rock mounds on the field started to melt from Flamethrower's heat. There was nowhere to hide—nowhere to even step.

"Way to go, Charizard!" Ash cheered.

"Blastoise, use Hydro Pump to cool the field down!" Gary hollered.

When the heat on the ground met the water from Hydro Pump, the entire battlefield was covered in a thick fog of steam. At first, Ash and Gary couldn't see what was going on.

"There they are!" The judge pointed.

Charizard and Blastoise were locked in hand-to-hand combat. The two Pokémon were so close, Blastoise couldn't aim its hydro cannons.

Blastoise dodged Charizard's harsh breath of Dragon Rage. So Charizard carried it up in the air.

"*Blastoise!*" Gary's Pokémon shouted, sinking its teeth into Charizard with Bite.

"*Charizaaard!*" it yelped.

"Don't give in!" Ash rallied. "Seismic Toss with everything you've got!"

"*Charrrrrizarrrrd!*" the Fire-type shouted as it tossed Blastoise back into the battlefield. When the dust cleared, Charizard and Blastoise were both on their feet. Charizard was ready to keep fighting.

"Blassssstoiiiise," Gary's Pokémon sighed, falling to its knees.

"The winner is Ash Ketchum from Pallet Town!" the judge announced.

"Pika!" Pikachu cheered, jumping up on Ash's shoulder.

All of Ash's friends surrounded him to congratulate him on his big win.

"Hey, thanks a lot, guys!" said Ash. But Gary strode off of the field before Ash could even thank him for the match.

Ash was happy about his win, but he was worried about not shaking Gary's hand after the battle. Rivalry aside, Ash knew Gary was an incredible Trainer, and if anything proved that, it had been this tournament.

That night, Gary sent Ash a message asking to meet him down by the lake. Ash was curious to see what his longtime opponent had to say.

"Here, this belongs to you. You earned it!" said Gary, extending the other half of the Poké Ball they'd split so long ago. "Take it, really."

"Thanks," Ash said.

"That battle today of ours was awesome! I don't even feel bad that I lost," Gary explained. "You beat me fair and square."

"You know, Gary, I learned a lot from battling you today," Ash said.

"Thanks! Well, I just wanted to let you know, I'll be rooting for you in the next round. Good luck!" Gary responded, reaching to shake Ash's hand.

"Thank you! Having your support means a lot to me, Gary," Ash replied.

Ash couldn't believe his rival had turned into a friend. Their Pokémon quests had taken them far from their home in Pallet Town, but they'd always be connected because of the bond of friendship they now shared.

COOL BATTLES IN JOHTO

ASH & MISTY FACE OFF AT THE WHIRL CUP

Ash and Misty are good friends, but that wasn't about to stop either one from battling at their best at the Whirl Cup. As a Water-type lover, Misty had a slight advantage at this Water-type Pokémon tournament. However, Ash is a fierce competitor, and he's always ready for a fun fight.

Misty chose her Pokémon first—Poliwhirl. Ash chose Totodile and had it make the first move with Water Gun. Poliwhirl surprised the crowd by jumping into the water, then hitting Totodile with a close-range Bubble and Double Slap combination. Totodile hit back with Skull Bash, but after a few of Poliwhirl's superstrong Double Slaps, it was unable to battle.

For his second Pokémon, Ash called on Kingler. Misty had Poliwhirl use Bubble again, but it was no match for the wave pool Kingler created with a few calculated Crabhammers. Kingler won the round!

Misty chose Psyduck as her second and final Pokémon, but it was already out of its Poké Ball, splashing around. Kingler easily surprised Psyduck with the tight pinch of Vice Grip. It wasn't looking good for Misty, but she wasn't about to give up. The minute Kingler eased its Vice Grip, Misty had Psyduck use Confusion. It was so powerful that it blasted Kingler away in one shot.

Misty turned it around, and fast, to win the round! Ash was knocked out of the Whirl Cup, but he was excited to watch his friend continue in the competition.

GOLDENROD CITY GYM

Goldenrod City Gym Leader Whitney is a bit of a dreamer, but her Miltank sure is top-notch. Ash found out what a tough competitor Miltank is when he challenged Whitney. It took out all three of Ash's Pokémon.

Of course, Ash refused to give up his dream of earning the Plain Badge. There was just one thing to do: train—not just hard, but smart, too.

Ash decided to visit Whitney's uncle Milton at his Miltank ranch just outside of town to learn as much as he could about the Milk Cow Pokémon. When Team Rocket interrupted his training with an attempt to steal Miltank, Ash called on Totodile to soak their robot and Pikachu to blast them off.

Whitney and Uncle Milton were very grateful for his help. So Ash asked Whitney for a rematch. After his experience on the ranch, Ash was prepared to fight the seemingly unstoppable Miltank.

At first, it seemed like Miltank's Rollout would win the match again, but Ash had Totodile and Pikachu use the same clever combination trick they'd used to defeat Team Rocket. First, Totodile dug ditches to derail Miltank. Then Pikachu zapped it in midair. Using this brilliant strategy, Ash finally won a match against Whitney.

Although it wasn't officially a Gym battle, Whitney was so impressed by Ash's skills, she awarded him his second Gym badge in Johto—the Plain Badge.

LEGENDARY POKÉMON OF JOHTO

ENTEI

According to myths, this Pokémon was born in an active volcano and is known for having flames hotter than magma.

RAIKOU

This Pokémon moves with the speed of lightning and has the power of electricity.

SUICUNE

A loner at heart, this Pokémon is said to have healing tears that can purify water.

HO-OH

Ho-Oh is the ancient guardian of the sky. A rainbow follows wherever this Pokémon flies.

LUGIA

This powerful Pokémon can start and stop a storm, and lives at the bottom of the sea.

MYTHICAL POKÉMON OF JOHTO

CELEBI

This Mythical Pokémon can control time. It traveled from the future and is known as the spirit of the forest.

HOENN

Pokémon battles aren't the only things that heat up Hoenn! This region is known for the hot springs next to Mt. Chimney, an active volcano that always looks like it's on the verge of erupting. If you're interested in visiting this lava hot spot, follow the big cloud of smoke to the center of the region.

Mt. Chimney isn't Hoenn's only famous volcano. Sootopolis City sits in the crater of a dormant volcano that's covered in water just up to the top. The only way to get to this scenic city is to take the ferry. The people there are used to climbing stairs to get everywhere, from the multi-tiered market to their split-level homes, which are all set into the side of the natural rock.

Sunny Hoenn is also known for offering plenty of shade, thanks to all the trees on the mainland. It's a region full of gorgeous forests.

HOENN FIRST PARTNER POKÉMON

MUDKIP

The Mud Fish Pokémon has a Mohawk that's cool to look at and works even better than eyes. Through this fin, the Water-type can sense its surroundings like a very advanced radar system. It picks up the slightest changes in the air and water, so there's no hiding from Mudkip.

MUDKIP EVOLVES INTO MARSHTOMP, THEN SWAMPER

TORCHIC

Don't underestimate the tiny Chick Pokémon. It might walk a little wonky, but its aim is on point. This Fire-type can hit an opponent with its 1,800-degree breath and give it a suit made of soot with the blaze of its fireballs.

TORCHIC EVOLVES INTO COMBUSKEN, THEN BLAZIKEN.

TREECKO

This Grass-type's feet are its hook—literally! The Wood Gecko Pokémon can scale a wall using the hooks it has tucked behind its toes. Look out for its tail, too, because it can pack a powerful wallop.

TREECKO EVOLVES INTO GROVYLE, THEN SCEPTILE.

PROFESSOR BIRCH

Friendly Professor Birch's lab is in Littleroot Town, but you're not likely to find him there. This free-spirited scholar specializes in Pokémon habitats. So he has to travel to them—whether they're up in trees, down by the water, atop mountains, or even buried deep in caves. Luckily, he likes to hike. And if you see a Jeep swerving around, that's probably Professor Birch. He's a highly respected researcher and a poorly graded driver.

Professor Birch might come off as a daydreamer, but he's actually listening for hints. He's very perceptive. He's so good at looking for clues to find a Pokémon's natural habitats that he often unlocks Pokémon mysteries and even discovers villains' hideouts along the way. In fact, it was Professor Birch who blew the lid off of Team Aqua.

Ash first met the professor when he tried to heal Pikachu after it got overcharged by a magnetic field. Like May and the other Trainers who get their first partner Pokémon from Professor Birch, Ash has found he can always count on the lovable hippie. He often runs into the professor in his travels through Hoenn because they're both always on the go, pursuing their dreams.

ASH'S POKÉMON IN HOENN

TAILLOW → SWELLOW

On their way to Rustboro City, Ash and his friends got hungry, and all they had left to eat was one chocolate chip cookie. Before they could divide it, Taillow swooped in and snagged the delicious treat. When Ash chased it down, he accidentally angered its entire flock.

Luckily, Brock joined Ash just in time to smooth things over by whipping up some of his patented yum for everyone. With a meal in its belly, the Normal-Flying-type decided to join Ash on his journey. It evolved into Swellow during the final round of a flying tournament, to cinch the win.

TREECKO → GROVYLE → SCEPTILE

Ash met his Treecko while it was fighting with its fellow Treecko. They were all living in a tree that was on the verge of dying, but this Treecko refused to give up on its home. When the tree finally split, spilling seeds to grow new trees, Treecko also decided to start a new life—and joined Ash on his travels. One of Ash's most powerful Pokémon in Hoenn, Treecko evolved into Grovyle and then Sceptile.

CORPHISH

Corphish burrowed through the beach, Ash's tent, and even Team Rocket. When Ash finally came face-to-face with this powerful Pokémon, he had Treecko use the patience training they'd been working on to catch the Water-type.

TORKOAL

When Ash spotted Torkoal in the Valley of Steel, it was being bullied by a bunch of Steel-type Pokémon. After protecting Ash's Pokémon friends, it earned Ash's respect. And after its Overheat knocked Steelix down, it earned all the Steel-types' respect. When they'd made it safely through the valley together, Torkoal decided it wanted to keep traveling with its new friend, Ash.

SNORUNT → GLALIE

Snorunt stole Ash's badge case, which started them off on the wrong foot. Then, when Snorunt ran up a hill to escape and ended up in a fierce blizzard, Ash wound up losing his footing trying to save the Ice-type from a terrible fall. The Snow Hat Pokémon built Ash a special igloo while it went for help. Later, Ash challenged Snorunt to a battle with Pikachu, and at last he caught his new pal. During some rigorous training with Ash, it evolved into Glalie in order to master Ice Beam.

MAY

Ten-year-old May was so excited to get her first partner Pokémon from Professor Birch, she was popping wheelies on her bike on the ride over to his lab. Adventure-loving May couldn't wait to travel the world as a Pokémon Trainer. However, she was more excited for all the different cities she'd get to visit than the Pokémon she'd see along the way. In fact, she's pretty squeamish when it comes to Pokémon, and finds many of them creepy.

May met Ash the very day she was supposed to get her first partner Pokémon. Professor Birch was in the forest, trying to help Ash rescue Pikachu, when Team Rocket showed up. Funnily enough, Team Rocket's robot drained Pikachu of its extra charge, healing the ill Pokémon. When Pikachu went to blast them off, its incredible power also burned May's bike—just like it had once done to Misty's ride. Who says lightning can't strike twice?

Although she was out one bike, May gained new pals in Ash and Pikachu. Afraid to travel alone, she offered to show them the way to Oldale Town. Soon her brother, Max, would join them on their journey, too.

May's travels have helped her see the world, but it's also given her the opportunity to search for who she really is. May is like a sponge—soaking it all in. Sometimes, her open mind allows her to fall for tall tales, but it's also how she discovered she had the makings of a cool Pokémon Coordinator.

May chose Torchic as her first partner Pokémon because it nuzzled her leg as soon as it came out of its Poké Ball. They've been best friends ever since. Along her journey, May helped her pal evolve into Combusken and eventually Blaziken.

TORCHIC

MAY'S POKÉMON

TORCHIC ➡️ COMBUSKEN ➡️  BLAZIKEN

 WURMPLE ➡️ SILCOON ➡️  BEAUTIFLY

 BULBASAUR ➡️ IVYSAUR ➡️ VENUSAUR

 SQUIRTLE ➡️ WARTORTLE

 MUNCHLAX

 EEVEE ➡️ GLACEON

 SKITTY

MAX

May's little brother sure thinks he knows it all. He's very book smart, but while traveling with his sister and Ash he figures out he has a lot more to learn—especially if he wants to fulfill his dream of becoming a Pokémon Trainer.

Max first met Ash when he came to earn the Balance Badge at the Petalburg City Gym. Gym Leader Norman encouraged his son to get his head out of his books and gain some real-life experience by following May and Ash on their travels.

At first, May didn't want to babysit her annoying little brother. She was embarrassed to have him tagging along, telling silly stories about her. Max may not have a way with people, but he proved to have a way with Pokémon.

Max isn't old enough to be a Trainer yet, but he helped a wild Poochyena evolve and befriended the Mythical Deoxys. Eventually, even May saw his potential to grow into a great Pokémon Trainer. Traveling brought them closer together. This brother and sister learned they could always depend on each other—and on their new buddy, Ash.

NORMAN

Max and May's dad is one of the most famous Gym Leaders in Hoenn. As the head of the Petalburg City Gym, Norman is constantly being challenged by Trainers who want the chance to battle him for the Balance Badge. But no matter what, he's always there for his kids. This pop often pops up to check in and help out Max, May, and Ash while they travel.

ASH'S REMATCH WITH NORMAN

After some time on the road, Max and May returned home with their pals Ash and Pikachu in tow. Ash was thrilled to be back in Petalburg City. Although he'd once tried and failed to earn the Balance Badge from Max and May's dad, Norman, he couldn't wait to challenge him to a rematch.

Inspired by Ash's spirit, Norman agreed to battle Ash one more time. It would be his second and last chance to earn the Balance Badge. The pressure was on, but Ash and Pikachu were ready!

In the stands, Max was revved up to root for his dad, since he'd never had the chance to see him battle.

"Okay, Ash, are you ready?" Norman asked.

"You bet!" Ash replied.

To start the three-on-three battle, Ash picked Pikachu.

"*Pika pika!*" it said, stepping onto the battlefield.

"Slakoth, I choose you!" Norman responded.

Ash was eager to show Norman how much he'd improved since their last battle, but he couldn't seem to land an attack. No matter how fast Pikachu tried to use Quick Attack or Iron Tail, Slakoth was always able to dodge.

"Wow, Pikachu's attacks keep missing the mark," May noted.

"No matter how slow or fast Ash attacks, Slakoth can squirm out of it," Brock explained. "That's the power of Slakoth's Hidden Power."

Frustrated, Ash decided to call back Pikachu after it got trapped in Slakoth's Blizzard. Cleverly, Norman had started the battle with a Pokémon that really took control.

"Torkoal, you're up!" Ash called.

Torkoal immediately turned up the heat with Flamethrower. Luckily, that move was so strong it won the round!

Max took the hit even harder than Slakoth had. "No way!" he cried in disbelief. "How could Daddy and Slakoth lose this one?"

Max was upset, but Norman congratulated Ash on his smart strategy.

"I'm quite impressed with that Flamethrower. You raised your Torkoal well," Norman told Ash.

Next, Norman chose Vigoroth, the Wild Monkey Pokémon. Ash had figured Norman was going to call on the Normal-type. So he had Torkoal start with Overheat. But when Vigoroth got its claws into Torkoal with Scratch, it was no longer able to battle.

"You battled your best, now you deserve some rest," Ash told his pal.

"Can you believe Vigoroth beat Torkoal with just one attack?!" Max raved from the stands.

Ash decided it was time for him to call on his best friend again—Pikachu!

"Pikachu!" it cheered, ready to get back in the battle.

Before Vigoroth could make a move, Pikachu unleashed Thunderbolt.

"Pikachuuuuuuu!" it shouted, using all its might.

Vigoroth tried Scratch again, but Pikachu stopped it with Iron Tail. It was an impressive move, but Norman had another trick up his sleeve.

"Vigoroth, use Flamethrower!" Norman directed.

"Vigooooorooooooooth!" it cried as it shot flames.

The battle had just heated up! But Pikachu was still determined to win. So Ash had it use Quick Attack to get close, and its static electricity to stop Vigoroth in its tracks.

"Vigooooh!" Norman's Pokémon yelped, trapped in Pikachu's Electric-type haze.

"Now, Pikachu, use Iron Tail!" Ash instructed.

"Piiiiikach-UUUUUUU!" it screamed as it used all its energy to finish the round with a wallop.

After that big blow, both Vigoroth and Pikachu were unable to battle. Now

Norman and Ash were both down to their last Pokémon pick.

Ash chose Grovyle, while Norman called on Slaking.

Ash knew his only chance at the Balance Badge was riding on this match. "Okay, Grovyle, I'm counting on you, buddy!"

"Grovyle!" it said, ready to go.

Grovyle started with a strong Bullet Seed pellet show.

"Slaking!" Norman's Pokémon replied, catching them in its mitts.

Next, Grovyle tried Leaf Blade, but not only did Slaking catch the green discs, it threw them right back at Grovyle.

"Slaking's hands are so strong, they're like two steel plates!" Brock cried.

"Talk about power!" Max gushed.

Then, Norman had Slaking use Focus Punch.

"Now's our chance! Quick, use Bullet Seed again," Ash directed.

Grovyle was able to hit Slaking, but now it was super angry.

"Slaaaaaking!" it bellowed, making the ground shake with Earthquake.

When angry Slaking added a forceful Hyper Beam, Grovyle fell to its knees. The match looked over.

"Grovyle, are you okay, buddy?" Ash asked.

"Grov grovyle!" it replied, ready for more. It charged up with Overgrow, strengthening the power of its Grass-type attacks.

"That's incredible!" Norman cried.

Slaking shook the battlefield again with Earthquake, but Grovyle kept jumping to avoid its power. Norman and Slaking tried to end the match with Focus Punch, but Ash saw an opportunity to strike.

"Go, Grovyle, give them a full-power Leaf Blade attack!" Ash called.

"Grov grovyle!" it shouted, scoring a direct hit with its discs.

Grovyle won the round—and Ash won the battle!

"Congratulations, Ash!" Norman said. "I haven't enjoyed a battle this much in a long time."

Norman held out his hand to offer Ash his fifth Gym badge in Hoenn, the Balance Badge. But before Ash could celebrate his win, Max ran out in tears.

"No way," Max muttered. "I can't believe Ash really beat Dad!"

May, Norman, Brock, and Ash chased after Max, but he'd locked himself in his room.

"Max, what's wrong?" May asked.

"Why did you have to lose, Daddy?" the boy cried. "You said you had a great time battling, but you lost. It doesn't make sense!"

"Gym Leaders don't work hard and hold battles just to keep winning," Brock said. "How would anyone get a badge if they did?"

"That doesn't mean it's okay to lose," Max said.

"Yes, it is!" Norman promised. "If you've battled hard and done your best, then defeat can end up being a great teacher of your strengths and weaknesses as a Trainer. It's a fun way to learn!"

Through the door, they could hear that Max wasn't crying anymore.

"Hey, Max? It's me, Ash," the Trainer said into the keyhole. "Look, if you want to keep that badge, it's okay, really! Thanks to that battle with your dad, I've learned a lot, too. And that's a lot more important than any badge!"

Click. The door opened again. Max was so moved by Ash's offer, he came back out. Norman, Ash, Brock, and May gave him a big hug.

But Max had one more question he needed answered. "Hey, Dad? When I'm old enough to be a Trainer, can I battle you for the Balance Badge, too?"

"Of course! It would be an honor," Norman said, smiling.

"Congratulations, Ash, you earned that badge," Max said.

"And someday, when you're a great Trainer, you will, too," Ash promised.

A DYNAMITE BATTLE FOR THE DYNAMO BADGE

Ash arrived in Mauville City with one thing on his mind: earning his third Gym badge in Hoenn. The local Gym leader, Wattson, was known for being a prankster and Electric-type expert. So Ash and Pikachu couldn't wait to battle him.

It was a bumpy ride on the way into the Mauville City Gym. The ground shook, rattled, and even roller-coastered—just like an amusement park. At the end of the ride, Wattson and Raikou greeted Ash and Pikachu. Ash had Pikachu use Thunderbolt and Iron Tail to win what he thought was the first round, but Raikou turned out to be a robot that zapped Pikachu right back. Raikou was just one of Wattson's tricks! Now for the real battle. Wattson picked his three Pokémon: Voltorb, Magnemite, and Magneton. Although Ash was traveling with plenty of Pokémon with a type advantage, Pikachu was raring to go! Ash's best pal proved itself on the battlefield by winning each round. Wattson could hardly believe it! Even Ash was amazed. Wattson awarded Ash the Dynamo Badge. The jolly Gym Leader was a little depressed that Pikachu had defeated his three Electric-types so easily.

After the battle, Pikachu wasn't feeling its best. So Ash decided to head over to see Nurse Joy. She diagnosed Pikachu with an overcharge. Suddenly, Ash realized the truth: The Raikou robot had shocked Pikachu with extra power, and that's how it was able to sweep the match with Wattson!

Ash and his friends ran out of the Pokémon Center to search for Wattson. First, the kids headed to his favorite place, the local power plant. There they found Wattson with his new Pokémon pal, Electrike.

Before Ash could say a word to Wattson, Team Rocket swooped in and captured Electrike and Pikachu! Wattson and Ash quickly teamed up to blast off Team Rocket.

After they battled the bad guys together, Ash tried to return the Dynamo Gym badge. But Wattson wouldn't take it. He said Ash deserved it for his honesty and for all his help freeing Electrike from Team Rocket.

Wattson returned to his Gym with Electrike. Ash wished Wattson well and continued on his journey, hoping that someday they would cross paths again.

LEGENDARY POKÉMON OF HOENN

GROUDON

Weighing in at over one ton, this Legendary Pokémon is a force of nature. It's known for holding power over volcanoes and magma—which is what the villains who worship it, Team Magma, take their name from. The lava Groudon controls causes water to evaporate, and when the lava cools, it forms new ground. Its powers directly oppose Kyogre, and the two have battled, but they have the same strength. So the balance between land and water has remained steady.

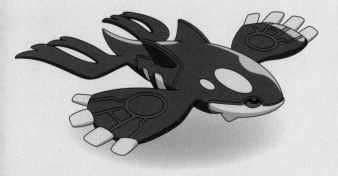

KYOGRE

The ruler of the sea, Kyogre is credited with covering the land with so much rain that oceans were created. Its power of water is so incredibly strong that there is a group of evil villains named Team Aqua who want to control the whole world with Kyogre's strength.

LATIAS

The glasslike feathers that cover its body refract light to alter Latias's appearance. It is the only Pokémon that possesses the knowledge to use Mist Ball.

LATIOS

This Legendary Pokémon possesses an incredible telepathic power to show friends things as if they are looking through its eyes.

RAYQUAZA

This Legendary Pokémon has only recently been discovered, because it lives in the ozone layer and has never touched down on the ground.

REGICE

Made of solid ice, not even fire can melt this frozen Legendary Pokémon.

REGIROCK

Made of solid rock, Regirock can piece itself back together with boulders it finds lying around.

REGISTEEL

The Legendary Iron Pokémon is made of metal.

MYTHICAL POKÉMON OF HOENN

DEOXYS

This alien, formed by a meteor, can change into four Formes: Normal, Speed, Defense, and Attack.

JIRACHI

Forget a fancy alarm clock. Unless it's woken by a voice of purity, this Mythical Pokémon prefers to stay asleep.

SINNOH

While traveling through Sinnoh, keep your eyes open for all the breathtakingly gorgeous natural beauty. Running right through the middle of the region is a mountain range with an incredible peak called Mt. Coronet.

If you're traveling up north, be sure to bring your sled! North Sinnoh is covered in a blanket of snow.

To the northwest is the region's biggest wilderness, Eterna Forest. It's easy to get lost in its lush greenery.

Throughout the region, there are many lovely lakes to camp by, but three are particularly special because Legendary Pokémon call them home. Mesprit lives in Lake Verity to the west. Uxie's habitat is Lake Acuity in the north. Azelf swims in Lake Valor to the east.

SINNOH FIRST PARTNER POKÉMON

CHIMCHAR

No one's gassier than Chimchar. Fueled by its stomach, the flame on its tail won't go out, not even in the rain. This Fire-type boasts an unstoppable blaze.

CHIMCHAR EVOLVES INTO MONFERNO, THEN INFERNAPE.

PIPLUP

This Water-type is a strong, independent Pokémon. It doesn't like to listen to anyone, so the Penguin Pokémon can prove to be a difficult first partner Pokémon.

PIPLUP EVOLVES INTO PRINPLUP, THEN EMPOLEON.

TURTWIG

The Tiny Leaf Pokémon loves to soak in the sun. It has two leaves on its head, but its whole body participates in photosynthesis. The shell on its back is actually tough as dirt because it is just that—hard soil.

TURTWIG EVOLVES INTO GROTLE, THEN TORTERRA.

PROFESSOR ROWAN

Sinnoh's head professor is an expert in Pokémon Evolution. He's dedicated his studies to the processes a Pokémon uses to evolve, and to their habits. To date, Rowan's data has him convinced that Pokémon are linked to one another by Evolution.

A brilliant mind, Rowan started his research even before Professor Oak. So it's no wonder Gary Oak has joined the esteemed Professor Rowan's studies at his lab in Sandgem Town. In fact, the first time Ash sees his old rival since the Silver Conference is at Professor Rowan's in Sinnoh.

Professor Rowan might seem tough and focused on his research, but deep down, he really cares about the Trainers he helps begin their journey. He even gave Dawn a Pokédex in her favorite color—pink!

DAWN

Have you ever heard the expression "History repeats itself"? Well, when Ash met Dawn, that sage saying came true! Ash and Pikachu befriended Dawn the same way they introduced themselves to Misty and May—Pikachu's big bolt of electricity fried her bike.

Dawn wants to be a top Pokémon Coordinator, just like her mom, Johanna. To remind her of her goal and her legacy, she carried her mother's first Contest Ribbon with her on her journey from her home in Twinleaf Town.

Dawn's motto is "No need to worry!" That is, unless her hair looks bad. If she's got a little frizz from one of Pachirisu's surprise Discharges, she'll have Piplup use Bubble Beam to smooth it out. Her little Water-type works better than a blow-dryer!

Speaking of hair, Dawn's been haunted by electric charges to her mane ever since she was a little girl. Back in her early school days, she hugged her class's Pokémon pals, Plusle and Minun, so tightly that they zapped her to escape. The electric charge made her hair sparkle with electric sparks, and she was nicknamed "Diamond Dandruff," or "Dee-Dee" for short. It's a name that embarrasses her to this day.

But no matter what you call her, Dawn is stylish from head to toe. In fact, her mom had to stop her from taking an entire suitcase full of clothes on her journey. To be fair, part of being a top Coordinator is looking fabulous on stage—and with her Pokémon, does she ever!

DAWN'S POKÉMON

PIPLUP

PACHIRISU

BUIZEL

BUNEARY

AIPOM ⇨ AMBIPOM

SWINUB ⇨ PILOSWINE ⇨ MAMOSWINE

CYNDAQUIL ⇨ QUILAVA

TOGEKISS

STARLY → STARAVIA → STARAPTOR

When Aipom accidentally knocked into a wild Starly in the woods, they started to fight. So Ash seized the opportunity to catch his first Pokémon pal in Sinnoh. Since then, Ash and Starly have been an incredible team. Ash really relied on this Normal-Flying-type and was not only able to help it evolve into Staravia and then Staraptor, but also learn the fierce move Brave Bird.

TURTWIG → GROTLE → TORTERRA

This Turtwig was the unofficial president of the forest. It ruled bravely—solving squabbles, caring for ill Pokémon, and fighting for Pokémon in distress, which is precisely how it met Ash.

When Team Rocket tried to take Pikachu, Turtwig stepped in to blast them off. Not only was it quick in battle, it healed quickly from injuries using Synthesis. After joining Ash on his journey, it evolved into Grotle, and then Torterra. No matter where they traveled, the Grass-type was always there to act as a peacemaker for its fellow Pokémon.

CHIMCHAR → MONFERNO → INFERNAPE

This Fire-type had a tough start with training. But the fire in its heart matches the blaze of its tail. Once it joined Ash's team, Chimchar found the friendship it was looking for, and it also evolved into Monferno and then Infernape.

BUIZEL

Originally part of Dawn's Contest crew, this Water-type proved it had a taste for battle. To help it fulfill its dream, Dawn and Ash arranged a trade, and Buizel joined Ash on his journey.

AIPOM

Aipom started out training for battles with Ash, but it kept showing its flair for performance. The Long Tail Pokémon is a total ham! Eventually, Dawn and Ash arranged a trade with Buizel so it could compete with Dawn in Pokémon Contests.

GLIGAR → GLISCOR

Slow at first, Gligar stood out as a weakling in its flock. But Ash saw potential in Gligar and spent a lot of time training with it. Eventually, their hard work paid off and Gligar evolved into Gliscor.

GIBLE

This Pokémon sure knows how to play hard to get. But Ash proved he would go the distance, even if that meant taking a fall off a cliff! Gible caught Ash in its chompers, and they were friends from that bite on.

This Dragon-Ground-type has a reputation for not being able to control its Draco Meteor blasts. They often land right on Ash, bringing lots of laughs to Ash's buddies during training.

PAUL

Coldhearted and calculating, Paul only cares about one thing—winning. He's not just Ash's rival; he's Ash's opposite.

Paul uses his Pokédex to check stats on every Pokémon he catches before deciding to keep it or not. In fact, when Ash first met Paul, he'd just caught three new Pokémon in a flock of wild Starly. However, Paul only held on to the strongest Starly and immediately released the other two. There is no room for weakness on his team. He's focused on strength and has impossibly high standards.

Just because Paul gives you a spot on his team doesn't mean you can stay there. Paul expects that his Pokémon will always bring their A games. Win or lose, if a Pokémon doesn't perform well, Paul will lash out and even possibly abandon them. He can be pretty cutthroat and cruel, but Paul would argue that his actions are purely logical. For Paul, being a Pokémon Trainer isn't about friendship, teamwork, or even fun. He doesn't care whom he hurts along the way as long as he gets his victory.

Ash is obsessed with convincing Paul of just how wrong his heartless battle strategy is. Unfortunately, the best Ash can seem to do in a battle against Paul is a draw.

ELEKID → ELECTABUZZ → ELECTIVIRE

MAGMAR → MAGMORTAR   NINJASK

LAIRON → AGGRON

GASTRODON   DRAPION   FROSLASS

THE HEARTHOME TAG BATTLE

Friendly Hearthome City hosts a famous Tag Battle Tournament that pairs Trainers up at random to battle together. Ash, Dawn, and Brock were all excited to meet a new friend and battle partner. But Ash already knew the guy he was slated to share the tournament with—his rival Paul!

"Of course, I had to be stuck with you," Paul complained. "Just make sure you don't get in my way!"

"Paul, that's no way to talk to your Tag Battle partner," Ash replied.

Pikachu tried to say hi to Paul's Pokémon pal Elekid.

"Elekid!" it responded, putting its paw out with a smile. But when Pikachu went to shake, Elekid zapped it instead!

"Pikachuuuu!" Ash's Pokémon was ready to blast Elekid back.

Ash jumped in and grabbed Pikachu before a battle broke out. He stopped the attack in time, but ended up taking the jolt instead.

"Whoa, Pikachu, you've gotten strong," cried Ash, his hair standing on end.

But Ash had a big problem. The Tag Battle was all about playing as a team to beat your opponents. But with a partner like Paul, who needed enemies?

Meanwhile, Paul began training with Chimchar.

"Chimcharrrrr!" it yelped, releasing a fiery blast. It had a powerful Flamethrower, but it couldn't control its aim. The flames shot right by Ash, who dodged the attack.

"A weak Flamethrower from a lame flame," Paul teased Chimchar.

"I thought it was great!" Ash replied. "Why don't we practice together to get that aim perfect?"

"We don't need your help," Paul shot back.

"But we're supposed to be a team! Why did you enter this competition anyway?!" Ash wondered.

"To meet Fire-types," Paul replied.

Ash wasn't sure what Paul meant by that. Then Brock reminded Ash about a time when Paul had used Pikachu's powerful Thunderbolt to supercharge Elekid.

"I bet he's trying the same strategy to fire up Chimchar!" Brock suggested.

"It makes sense, but I sure don't like it," Ash replied.

After Brock and his partner, Holly, won their match, it was time for the final battle of the first round. Ash and Paul stepped onto the field.

"Ready, Pikachu?" Ash asked.

"Pikachu!" it cheered.

"Chimchar, stand by," Paul instructed his Pokémon.

Ash and Paul's opponents chose the Spitfire Pokémon, Magmar, and Rhydon, the Drill Pokémon. It would be a tough match.

Ash had Pikachu start out on the offensive with Thunderbolt.

"Pikachuuuuu!" It was a direct hit, but Rhydon didn't seem fazed.

"Huh?!" Ash said, confused.

"Rhydon used Lightning Rod, which can absorb any Electric-type move," Brock explained.

"Ugh, how did you not know that?! You're just in my way," Paul complained.

Magmar made the next move—Lava Plume. The field around it was covered in flames. Cruel Paul had Chimchar jump right into the blaze.

"Now, use Flamethrower!" Paul commanded.

"Chimchaaaaarrrrrr!" it shouted, unleashing an extra-strong attack. Lava Plume had it all fired up.

But Rhydon was so strong that it easily blocked Chimchar's Flamethrower. Then Rhydon responded with Hammer Arm.

"Rhydooooon!" it screamed, charging after Chimchar.

Pikachu stopped Rhydon in its tracks with a whack of Iron Tail.

Rhydon worked up a wall of water for Surf. Soon it was riding it into Pikachu and Chimchar.

"Flame Wheel, let's go," Paul told Chimchar.

"That's crazy!" Dawn cried. "Chimchar is going to get creamed."

Ash was worried about Paul's Pokémon pal, even if Paul wasn't. Suddenly, he remembered a battle in which his friend Zoey had Glameow cut through Shellos's solid swirls of water.

"Pikachu, use Iron Tail!" Ash shouted.

"Piiiiiiikaaaachuuuuuu!" it screamed, using Iron Tail to cut the wall of water. With the water split, Pikachu landed a direct hit on Rhydon.

"Rhydooooonnnnn," it sighed, unable to battle.

"That was great!" Brock cheered.

Magmar was still standing. So Ash had Pikachu use Volt Tackle.

"Magmaaaaar!" it shouted, swinging Fire Punch.

Pikachu and Magmar were locked in place. Their attacks were equal in strength!

Then Chimchar used Dig to sneak up on Magmar. Now Magmar was unable to battle, too. Pikachu and Chimchar had won the round!

But Paul wasn't happy—he still had to deal with Ash. "From now on, stay out of my face," he snapped.

"Face it, Paul! We have to work together as a team," Ash pleaded.

But Paul wouldn't listen. Both Trainers practiced for the second round alone.

While Ash was training with Turtwig, Pikachu, and Aipom, he spotted a bright blast of Flamethrower in the forest. When he went to check it out, he found Paul practice-battling with all his Pokémon—except it wasn't a fair fight. Paul's Ursaring, Elekid, Torterra, and Murkrow were all directing their attacks right at Chimchar.

"Hey, Paul, what's going on here?" Ash asked.

"Now Flamethrower!" Paul instructed, ignoring Ash.

Chimchar was so overwhelmed and exhausted, it accidentally fired its Flamethrower right at Ash. Ash was knocked to the ground by the sheer power of the attack.

"Chimchar!" it apologized, running over to make sure Ash was okay.

"Wow, you just keep getting stronger!" Ash complimented Chimchar.

Paul called Chimchar back to the battle. He wasn't done training with it.

"Why are you so hard on Chimchar?" Ash asked Paul.

"You don't get it," Paul replied. "I needed Chimchar to be struck by that Surf today to make it stronger."

"But what if it had lost?" Ash replied.

"Then it would have been useless to me," Paul said. "I'm trying to make it strong enough to be on my team. This is what Chimchar wants."

"There are other ways to get stronger, Chimchar. You don't have to do it the hard way." Ash tried to reason with the Fire-type.

"Come on, Chimchar, don't listen to that loser!" Paul said, striding away with his other Pokémon.

Chimchar kept training late into the night. It dodged Ursaring's Hammer Arm, but when Torterra caught it in Leaf Storm, Murkrow scored a direct hit with Sky Attack. Chimchar was taking a beating from all sides.

"Now Flamethrower!" Paul demanded.

But Chimchar couldn't muster the strength to fight back. It fell over, too tired to keep battling.

"Elekid, wake it up with Thunder," Paul commanded.

Elekid fired its electric attack, but when the light cleared, Pikachu was standing in front of Chimchar, protecting it!

"Piiikachu!" it reprimanded Paul and Elekid.

"You've done more than enough," Ash added. "I'm taking Chimchar to the Pokémon Center to rest."

"Be my guest," Paul sneered.

The next day, Paul picked up Chimchar and took it back to the arena. Ash and Paul were up again—and Paul chose Chimchar. So Ash called on Turtwig, but his heart wasn't in winning the battle. Ash was focused on one thing.

"Whatever you do, make sure you protect Chimchar!" Ash called.

"Turtwig!" it promised.

Their opponents chose their Pokémon for the battle: Metagross and Zangoose.

"Chimchaaaaaar!" The little Fire-type's jaw dropped when it saw Zangoose.

But Paul wouldn't let it back down. And neither would Zangoose. It was already headed straight for the Fire-type.

"Chimchar, Flamethrower!" Paul commanded.

But Chimchar was frozen with fear. So Ash had Turtwig fire Leaf Blade at Zangoose, but it quickly deflected the discs.

"Use Dig!" Paul told Chimchar.

When Chimchar tried to sneak up on Metagross, Zangoose surprised it with a punch.

"Chimchar, use Flame Wheel on Turtwig," Paul commanded.

"Chimchar," it replied, shaking its head.

"Do it!" Paul demanded. Chimchar used Flame Wheel, and its fireball hit Zangoose, Metagross, and its own teammate, Turtwig!

"Turtwig, are you okay?" Ash cried.

"Turt turt turtwig," it said, struggling to get back on its feet.

"What's wrong with you?!" Ash yelled at Paul.

Before Chimchar could get another Flame Wheel going, Zangoose trapped it in Crush Claw.

"Use Flamethrower!" Paul instructed.

"Zaaaangoooooose!" Zangoose snarled at Chimchar.

"Chimchar!" it cried out in fear.

"Turtwig, you've got to help Chimchar!" Ash cried.

"Turtwig wig wig!" Ash's Grass-type shouted, shooting Razor Leaf at Zangoose.

It worked, but Turtwig looked tired.

Zangoose and Metagross went on the offensive, but before they could hit Turtwig, Chimchar jumped in front of its pal.

"Chimcharrrrrrr!" it screamed, shooting fire to deflect their attacks. But Chimchar could only hold them off for so long.

"Hurry, Paul, give Chimchar its next move," Ash said.

Paul turned his back on the match. So Ash stepped up. "Chimchar, use Flamethrower!"

"Chiiiiimchaaaaarrrrrr!" it screamed, giving Flamethrower all the fire it had.

In that incredible heat, Metagross was unable to battle. And watching Chimchar inspired Turtwig to get back into the match.

"All right, Turtwig!" Ash cheered. He had Turtwig use a combination of Razor Leaf and Tackle to win the round.

"Wow!" Ash celebrated. "I can't tell you how great you both were, Chimchar and Turtwig."

But what seemed like a victory quickly turned into a loss. Outside the arena, Paul released Chimchar.

"I'm done wasting time with you," Paul told the Fire-type.

"You're giving up Chimchar?" Ash asked, confused.

"Obviously, I need to get a stronger Fire-type," Paul said.

"Chimchar," it whimpered, walking off into the forest alone.

"Wait, Chimchar." Ash chased after it. "Come with us! We'll have a blast together."

But before Chimchar could join his new friends, Team Rocket swooped in on their hot-air balloon and grabbed it!

"Don't worry, Chimchar, we'll get you out of there!" Ash promised.

"Chimchar," it replied with determination. The little Fire-type was so inspired by Ash's devotion that it blasted off Team Rocket all by itself!

As Chimchar fell from the hot air balloon, Ash dove to catch it in his arms.

"Chimchar!" it cheered, jumping with joy.

But Ash and Chimchar weren't rid of Paul just yet. They still had another round to go at the Hearthome Tag Battle Tournament. The final match was Dawn and Buizel with her partner, Conway, and Heracross versus Ash with Chimchar and Paul with Elekid.

No surprise, Paul refused to work with Ash again.

"Look, Paul, if we don't start working together, we're going to lose this thing," Ash said.

"So what if we do?" Paul responded.

Heracross attacked Elekid with Feint, and then threw it with its horn.

"Heracrossss!" it shouted, using Megahorn.

"Elekiiiiiid!" Paul's Pokémon countered with Thunder Punch.

The two Pokémon were locked in evenly matched attacks. When it could no longer maintain its attack, Elekid was thrown to the ground.

"Chimchar?" Ash's new Pokémon asked Elekid if was okay.

Elekid was embarrassed about looking weak. It got so angry with Chimchar for caring that a bright yellow light surrounded it. When Paul's Pokémon reappeared, it had evolved into Electabuzz!

"Electabuzz!" it shouted, ready to keep battling.

"Use Thunder," Paul commanded.

"Chimchar, add Flamethrower!" Ash shouted.

The bolt of light, combined with the flash of fire, covered the other half of the battlefield in a big explosion.

"Whoa!" Ash said, amazed.

Buizel and Heracross were down for the count! Ash and Paul had won the Hearthome Tag Battle Tournament!

"See, Chimchar, you're the best!" Ash cheered. He turned to Paul. "Wow, everything totally changed for the better after Elekid evolved into Electabuzz!"

"Actually, Electabuzz won this round. Chimchar's Flamethrower couldn't even knock

Heracross out. If it wasn't for Thunder, you would have lost. You're so pathetic. You two deserve each other," Paul replied.

"Talk all you want, Paul. I know you were awesome out there, Chimchar!" Ash said, petting his new Pokémon pal.

"*Chimchar!*" it said, smiling.

At the closing ceremony, Ash and Paul were presented with their awards in front of a whole arena of fans.

"All right, we got a calming Soothe Bell!" Ash exclaimed.

Thwap! Paul tossed his Soothe Bell right at Ash.

"I have no need for this," Paul said, striding away.

With his new Pokémon pal, Chimchar, in tow, Ash was excited for his next battle. Dawn, Brock, and Ash decided to head out to Veilstone City together. Ash had big plans there—to earn his third Gym badge in Sinnoh with the help of his friends, both new and old.

CYNTHIA

Cynthia is a true force to be reckoned with on the battlefield. She's renowned throughout the Pokémon world for being the Sinnoh region's League Champion. In other words, she's the toughest Trainer to beat in Sinnoh. In fact, winning a battle against her seems impossible—just ask Sinnoh's Elite Four members, Flint, Aaron, Lucian, and Bertha. With her trusty Garchomp by her side, she uses her incredible skills to protect Sinnoh's mythical treasures, like the Lustrous Orb.

Despite her important position, Cynthia always finds time to give young Trainers like Ash guidance. She even accepts battle challenges from Paul and Iris. Cynthia is as caring as she is noble. A beacon of light and wisdom, she trained her way to the top, and there's a reason she's still number one.

GARCHOMP

Cynthia's go-to Pokémon, Garchomp, is large and takes charge of every battle. It's known for its powerful attacks like Draco Meteor, Giga Impact, and Dragon Rage.

LOOKER

Look out, crooks, Looker is a well-known crime-stopper and special agent of the International Police. He's hot on Team Galactic's tail in Sinnoh, and Team Plasma's tail in Unova. So Ash and his friends offer Looker a hand in foiling any evil plot they can.

LEGENDARY POKÉMON OF SINNOH

CRESSELIA

This Legendary Pokémon, which brings happy dreams, is said to be a symbol of the crescent moon.

DIALGA

According to myth, time began when this Legendary Pokémon was born. It is said to have the ability to control time.

GIRATINA

As punishment for its violence, Giratina was banished to another dimension, where everything is distorted and reversed.

HEATRAN

Heatran lives in caves carved out by volcanic eruptions. Its feet can dig into rock, so it can walk on walls and ceilings.

PALKIA

Palkia possesses the power to distort space. It lives in a parallel dimension with its counterpart, Dialga.

REGIGIGAS

According to legend, Regigigas built smaller models of itself out of rock, ice, and magma. It's so enormous that it could tow an entire continent behind it.

THE TRIO OF LAKE GUARDIANS

AZELF

Known as "the Being of Willpower," Azelf calls Lake Valor home.

MESPRIT

According to legend, "the Being of Emotion" lives in Lake Verity and taught humans the depths of sorrow, pain, and joy.

UXIE

Uxie is rumored to live in Lake Acuity and is considered "the Being of Knowledge."

MYTHICAL POKEMON OF SINNOH

ARCEUS

People in Sinnoh believe that Arceus emerged from its Egg into complete nothingness, and then shaped the world and everything in it.

DARKRAI

Darkrai defends its territory by sending intruders into a deep sleep, where they are tormented by terrible nightmares.

MANAPHY

Manaphy possesses the power to form close bonds with any Pokémon, no matter what kind.

PHIONE

Phione gather in large groups and drift on the currents of warm seas. They always return home, no matter how far they have traveled.

SHAYMIN

This Mythical Pokémon has two Formes: Sky and Land. Although they both possess the ability to purify toxins, the two are total opposites. Bashful Land Forme can hide in a field of Gracedia, which are wildflowers native to Sinnoh. But eventually, Land Forme will change into the bold Sky Forme.

UNOVA

Whether you're looking to retreat into the forest or find yourself in the middle of a busy city, Unova is the perfect region for you!

Go gallery-hopping in artsy Nacrene City. Stroll through the shops in fancy Striaton City. Catch a game at the big stadium or ride the giant Ferris wheel in sparkling Nimbasa City. Or, if you dream of becoming a movie star, head to the studios in Virbank City.

Unova also boasts natural wonders. Hike through Pinwheel Forest, which is brimming with beautiful trees and wild Pokémon. Ride down to relaxing Undella Town to swim in the crystal-blue sea, and you might just spot the Champion of Sinnoh. Cynthia has a vacation villa there.

Unova is a place that has something for everyone! There are not many Pikachu in the region, so everyone is thrilled to see Ash and his best pal. No one can resist challenging the rare Pokémon to a battle!

UNOVA FIRST PARTNER POKÉMON

TEPIG

A feisty Fire-type, Tepig always has its head in the game—its nose is built for battle. Fireballs can shoot out of the Fire Pig's nostrils. This comes in handy on the field—and it's also useful when it's time to cook dinner.

TEPIG EVOLVES INTO PIGNITE, THEN EMBOAR.

SNIVY

A little bit of sunlight will supercharge this Grass-type's attacks, but it's always got plenty of brainpower. Smart Snivy is great at battle strategy and has two long vines that can swing, slap, and wrap up an opponent.

SNIVY EVOLVES INTO SERVINE, THEN SERPERIOR.

OSHAWOTT

Oshawott's scalchop—the pretty shell on its belly—isn't stuck there. The Water-type can chuck it in battle or even slice open a berry with its sharp edge. The scalchop is more than just decoration for the Sea Otter Pokémon—it's protection.

OSHAWOTT EVOLVES INTO DEWOTT, THEN SAMUROTT.

PROFESSOR JUNIPER

Although she's young, Professor Juniper has earned a reputation for being one of the most important Pokémon researchers. The focus of her studies is Pokémon origins, but she's also obsessed with technology. This handy professor has a knack for creating incredible machines to help with her research.

Perhaps her two most important technological advances are the Pokémon Trading Device, which evolves and exchanges Pokémon during a battle, and the Pokémon Restoration Machine, which brought the ancient Archen back to life from a fossil.

PROFESSOR CEDRIC JUNIPER

Make sure when you're looking up Professor Juniper that you've got the right one, because there are two! Professor Cedric Juniper is Professor Juniper's dad. But he's not the kind of professor who studies in a lab. He prefers field research, and he's an expert on Unova's ancient ruins.

Professor Cedric is hard to find and hard to follow. Wait until you're sure he's finished each sentence before moving a muscle, because he speaks in backward sentences that can often be misleading. And frankly, he loves being misleading, because it can lead to even more adventure.

PIDOVE

This Normal-Flying-type is the first Pokémon Ash caught in Unova, with the help of his pal Pikachu—and not a moment too soon. When Team Rocket swooped in to steal Pikachu, it was Pidove who fought them off. From then on, Ash knew he could count on Pidove. Together, they stopped a Venipede stampede and earned the important Jet Badge. They're such an incredible team, Pidove soon evolved into Tranquill and then Unfezant.

OSHAWOTT

Ash didn't catch Oshawott—it caught up with him. The warm Water-type befriended Ash. Then, after spending a few days together, Oshawott asked to join his team. But when Ash went to toss his Poké Ball, it became clear that this Oshawott was the same one he'd met at Professor Juniper's lab. It had snuck out to follow him on his journey.

Ash immediately called Juniper to let her know Oshawott was A-OK. Delighted to hear that Oshawott was happy, Juniper gave Ash its Poké Ball so the two could keep traveling together. But Oshawott still likes to sneak out of its Poké Ball whenever it hears there's a chance to battle!

SANDILE

Supercool Sandile never takes off its shades. It looks tough, but this Desert Croc Pokémon is actually a total softy. Ash met it when it was using Dig to warn people at a resort of a coming natural disaster—nearby geysers were about to blow.

After teaming up with Ash, Sandile wanted to battle Pikachu. It was such an amazing match that it evolved into Krokorok. As part of Ash's team, it evolved again—into Krookodile.

ROGGENROLA

When Team Rocket captured a clan of Roggenrola to power their new weapon, one escaped and called on Ash for help. Always ready to do right, Ash and Roggenrola worked together to save the Rock-types, and they've been together ever since. While battling for the Quake Badge, Roggenrola evolved into Boldore to win the round.

SNIVY

The way to Snivy's heart is through its stomach! Snivy first saw—or rather smelled—Ash and his friends when Cilan was cooking up a delicious lunch. Sneaky Snivy stole a taste and disappeared like a ninja.

Ash was so in awe of this Pokémon's skill, he made it his mission to catch it—which was easier said than done. Slippery Snivy is always able to escape, when it saw what a good friend Ash was to his Pokémon, it wanted to be his pal, too!

SCRAGGY

Hatched from an Egg Ash received as a gift, Scraggy was born to battle! With its first words, it challenged Pikachu to a match. Unfortunately, its determination was stronger than its attacks. But that didn't stop Scraggy from trying to fight every Pokémon it met!

SEWADDLE

When Ash spotted Sewaddle in Pinwheel Forest, he was so impressed by its strength that he got his whole crew lost in the woods chasing after it. The Trainer and Pokémon might not have seemed like a good match at the start, but once Sewaddle saw what a caring Trainer Ash was, it wanted to be caught.

Always there to help a Pokémon in need, Ash saved Sewaddle from being kidnapped, and even shared his food with the wild Sewing Pokémon. From then on, the two were a great team. Sewaddle first evolved into Swadloon while battling Bug-type expert Burgh for the Insect Badge. Then it became Leavanny while practicing for another Gym battle.

TEPIG

When Ash first discovered Tepig in Don George's storeroom, it looked like an Umbreon because it was completely covered in black soot. When Ash got close to Tepig, he felt bad for the poor Pokémon, who'd been abandoned by a callous Trainer.

After a good meal and a little TLC, Tepig felt much better—and decided to join Ash on his journey.

PALPITOAD

While swimming to the bottom of a lake in search of Remeyo Weed to heal his sick Pokémon, Ash was attacked by Palpitoad. The Vibration Pokémon was just trying to protect its home. But now Ash needed protection!

Oshawott had been struggling with battling underwater because it was afraid to open its eyes. But when it saw Ash in trouble, it finally worked up the courage to face its fear. Not only did Oshawott land Aqua Jet to win the battle, Ash was able to catch Palpitoad.

CILAN

Tall Cilan has a green bow tie and hair to match. One of three triplets who run the restaurant/ Gym in Striaton City, Cilan knows Pokémon as well as he knows good cooking. That's because he's studied hard to become a Class A Pokémon Connoisseur and help Trainers build their friendships with Pokémon.

When Ash wanted to battle for the Trio Badge, he had his pick of the three Gym Leader brothers—Cilan, Cress, or Chili. Ash was the first Trainer to challenge not just one brother, but all three! Cilan was so impressed that he decided to join Ash on his journey through Unova.

You can take the guy out of the Gym/restaurant, but you can't take the restaurant out of the guy. Cilan still sees the world as a delicious dish, and he's constantly making food-related comparisons. Luckily for his traveling companions, it isn't just all talk. Cilan is also an excellent chef.

CILAN'S POKÉMON

DWEBBLE

PANSAGE

IRIS

Iris grew up in the Village of Dragons—a town obsessed with Dragon-types. So it's no wonder her dream is to become a Dragon Master.

Unlike most Trainers, who get their first partner Pokémon from professors, Iris received Axew from her village's elder. Ever since, she's been ready to challenge anyone and everyone she meets to a battle—even her school principal, Dragon-type expert Drayden. When she lost that match, she rebelled by leaving Drayden's Opelucid Academy to travel around Unova and train.

But Drayden is still keeping an eye on Iris—he has big plans for her. Drayden hopes that someday Iris will take his place as the Opelucid City Gym Leader and keeper of the Legend Badge.

Until then, she's got a lot to learn! Iris acts likes she knows it all, and she loves to tell Ash he's "such a kid." But she's happy to join Ash on his journey through Unova. And she has an unusual way of getting from place to place—Iris loves to climb trees and swing on vines.

IRIS'S POKÉMON

DRILBUR ⇨ EXCADRILL

EMOLGA

AXEW

DRAGONITE

TRIP

Cold and calculating, Trip is one tough competitor. He thinks everything and everyone is just "basic." So he doesn't waste time making friends.

Trip loves to talk trash, but he often shows he has the talent to back it up. Ash met Trip the day Trip received his first partner Pokémon. As Trip was leaving Professor Juniper's lab, he was already bragging that he was the best. Even though he'd never so much as practiced with his first partner Pokémon, Snivy, Trip was sure he'd beat Ash in a battle. And the craziest part is, he did!

Trip dreams of beating Alder and becoming the Unova League Champion someday. Until then, he's not going to stop—unless it's to take every opportunity to insult Ash.

TRIP'S POKÉMON

VANILLITE LAMPENT

SNIVY ⇒ SERVINE ⇒ SERPERIOR

FRILLISH TRANQUILL

TIMBURR ⇒ GURDURR ⇒ CONKELDURR

ALDER

The charismatic Unova League Champion is always in the public eye. Adoring fans trail his every move, and Alder always has time to give out advice and sign autographs—although he often gets his fans' names wrong. Just ask Ashton—or rather, Ash. But Alder has so much wisdom to pass on, no one seems to mind when he slips up on a name or two. To his credit, he never forgets a face!

Alder is a kindhearted hero who cares deeply about people and Pokémon. He's so magnetic, even Trip adores Alder. After meeting him at a young age, Trip considers him a mentor—although Trip has grown up to be his complete opposite.

Alder is lighthearted and always laughing, but he takes his job as Champion very seriously. He is on a nonstop adventure that can leave him exhausted, but it certainly keeps him happy. And he is happy to share that joy with everyone!

ASH VS. ALDER, THE UNOVA LEAGUE CHAMPION

Before leaving Nimbasa City, Ash, Pikachu, Brock, and Iris decided to take a stroll through Performer's Square to check out the cool street magicians, break dancers, and musicians. As they were taking in the sights, they recognized the only face around that wasn't smiling—Trip.

Before rivals Ash and Trip could even say hello, they had their Gym badges out, ready to compare.

"Ta-da! I have four," Ash bragged.

But inside Trip's case, there were already five.

"It's the difference in our skill levels. Basic stuff," Trip scoffed.

Insulted, Ash immediately challenged Trip to a battle. But Trip had a different challenger in mind for that day—Alder, the Unova League Champion, who also happened to be Trip's personal hero. Trip had met Alder when he was a little boy, and he still remembered that day perfectly.

Little Trip had told Alder that someday he wanted to battle him and win, so he could become the Champion. Impressed by his spirit and ambition, Alder gave him the advice that changed his life.

"You should battle a lot; then you'll become strong," Alder advised.

Since then, Trip had focused on strength above all else. He finally felt ready to battle his hero, and rumor had it Alder was hanging around Performer's Square.

Just then, the sound of a big belly laugh cut through the crowd.

"I know that laugh!" Trip cried, spotting Alder. "Look, there he is!"

Alder was hard to miss—his personality was as big as he was! The League Champion was a gentle giant with long red hair, a Poké Ball bead necklace, and a laid-back attitude. He was a huge celebrity in Unova.

Trip hurried to catch up with the Champion.

"Hi, Alder, we only met once, when I was a kid . . ." Trip said, trying to jog the Champion's memory.

"Right, I remember. You're Tristan!" Alder replied.

But before Trip could correct him, Ash had challenged Alder to a battle.

"Hey! Cool your jets. Alder is going to battle me!" Trip whined.

"Don't worry; I'll battle both of you," Alder promised.

Thinking strategically, Trip let Ash go first so he could study Alder's battle style before it was his turn.

"Now, Bouffalant, let's go!" Alder chose his Pokémon.

Bouffalant is known as the Bash Buffalo Pokémon because of its super-hard Headbutt. Its poufy hair is said to soften the blow of attacks against its head.

Ash called on his best friend, Pikachu. In this match, it looked like no one had the type advantage.

"Pikachu!" the Electric-type called, ready to battle.

"Have fun getting creamed!" Trip teased.

"I'll show you! Pikachu, use Thunderbolt," said Ash, starting the battle.

"Piiiikaaaachuuuu!" it yelled, unleashing a blast of light.

Bouffalant was completely unfazed by the strong Electric-type attack. And even stranger than Bouffalant's relaxed response was Alder's. Ash waited for Bouffalant to make a move, but it didn't.

"Okay; you snooze, you lose. Pikachu, use Quick Attack!" called Ash, to keep the battle going.

But again, Bouffalant seemed to feel nothing, and Alder said nothing.

"This must be the Champion's special battle flavor," Cilan suggested.

So Ash decided to have Pikachu try Iron Tail, and then Electro Ball.

"Piiiiikachuuuuu!" it shouted, giving the move its all.

"Bouff," Alder's Pokémon said, shaking it off with its big pouf of hair.

This was shaping up to be the weirdest battle Ash had ever fought. No matter what he and Pikachu tried, Alder didn't say a thing.

"Wait a second, I think the Champion is snoring!" Cilan cried. He was right—Alder had actually fallen asleep!

Cilan, Trip, and Iris went over to Alder, who was leaning up against a tree.

"Zzzzzzzzz," Alder snored.

"No way!" Trip said. "Come on, Alder, wake up!"

Alder jumped up. He apologized and sprang right back into action.

"Bouffalant, Head Charge!" Alder commanded. "Now, let's get to it!"

The Bash Buffalo Pokémon was a little annoyed that Alder had fallen asleep, too. It started racing toward Pikachu, then surprised everyone by turning around to hit his Trainer instead.

"Ha!" Alder laughed, petting his Pokémon pal. "I deserved that. By the way, that was an extraordinary Head Charge—just what I'd expect from you."

"Bouffalaaant," it sighed, forgiving Alder.

Alder decided to forfeit the match. He was too tired to keep battling. Instead, he offered to take everyone out to dinner.

"But you promised you'd battle me!" Trip complained.

"Come on, have a heart! If you're determined never to change your mind, then why have one?" Alder replied.

"Fine. Forget the battle," Trip said. "But just so you know, I have gotten strong like you told me to do."

"I told you to get strong?" Alder said, confused.

"Yeah, you told me strength was the most important thing in battle!" Trip shouted, frustrated with his hero.

"Hmmm, I wouldn't say that strength is most important," Alder responded thoughtfully.

"Talking to you is a waste of time. I'm going to prove I'm right by winning. With my strength, I'm going to be the real Champion." Trip stormed off.

"Well, it helps to enjoy life, too!" Alder shouted after him. "Geez, what's gotten into that guy?!"

Just then, Officer Jenny pulled up on her motorcycle. "Am I glad I found you, Alder," she said.

A gigantic wild Gigalith was trampling through town. Gigalith is so strong that the energy stored in its core can destroy a whole mountain. Officer Jenny was hoping the Champion could stop the Compressed Pokémon before it did some real damage.

Ash, Iris, Cilan, and Officer Jenny all wanted to battle Gigalith to stop it, but Alder wouldn't hear it.

"Hold on; you just leave this to me!" Alder promised. "If I fail, I'll let you step in. In the meantime, step back."

Officer Jenny and the kids stepped aside.

Alder slowly approached Gigalith with a Berry. Perhaps Gigalith was just hungry?

"Giga!" Gigalith said, angrily knocking Alder over with Headbutt.

"Okay, I guess that's my cue! Go, Herdier," Officer Jenny responded, calling on her Pokémon deputy.

"Wait! Bouffalant, make sure Herdier doesn't attack," Alder instructed. "I've got this. That Headbutt was a good thing—now I know what's gotten into Gigalith!" The Champion challenged Gigalith to attack again.

"Huh?!" Ash, Officer Jenny, Cilan, and Iris said, completely confused.

Using all its might, Gigalith charged toward Alder once more. What was the Champion thinking?

"Gigaaaa!" Gigalith screamed, running right up to Alder.

Not a moment too soon, Alder made his strategic move.

"Hi-ya!" Alder shouted, grabbing its foot when it got close. "Gotcha!"

Alder stopped the giant Pokémon in its tracks. Then the Champion flipped up its foot and pulled out a sharp nail stuck near its toes. Gigalith hadn't been on a rampage—it was just running around senselessly from pain.

"Pain can be very upsetting. No wonder you lost control," Alder said.

"Giga gigalith," it sighed with relief.

Gigalith's attitude quickly transformed from pure anger to pure gratitude. Attacking an injured Pokémon would have been cruel. Alder had been brave enough and smart enough to take a closer look and find out the real problem.

"Wow," Ash said, impressed. "No wonder he's the Champion!"

If only Trip had been there to learn once again from Alder, he would have seen that strength isn't always the best strategy. Compassion can be even more powerful!

COBALION

Like its body, Cobalion's heart is tough as steel. Legends say that in the past, it stood up for its fellow Pokémon and protected them from harmful people.

KYUREM

When the freezing energy inside Kyurem leaked out, its entire body froze. According to legend, it can only become whole with help from a hero who will bring truth or ideals.

TERRAKION

According to legend, Terrakion once attacked a mighty castle to protect its Pokémon friends. It knocked down a giant wall with the force of its charge.

VIRIZION

Legends say that Virizion can move so swiftly that its opponents are left bewildered. Its horns are lovely and graceful—and as sharp as blades.

RESHIRAM

The Vast White Pokémon might look ice-cold, but it's actually so hot it can instantly turn things to ash and cause the temperature of the entire world to rise.

ZEKROM

The Deep Black Pokémon disguises itself in thunderclouds so it can fly through the sky completely undetected. However, with a shock of the electric generator in its tail, it can announce its presence. It is so strong that it once temporarily took out the power and computer system in Professor Juniper's lab.

THE THREE POWERS OF NATURE

LANDORUS

With the touch of its tail, the Abundance Pokémon can transform any dirt into a field of crops bigger and fuller than any farmer could have grown.

THUNDURUS

Each of the six spikes on the Bolt Strike Pokémon's tail can shoot lightning.

TORNADUS

The Cyclone Pokémon can stir up quite a windstorm with the tap of its tail or by flying through the sky at two hundred miles per hour.

GENESECT

This Mythical Pokémon is three hundred million years old. Team Plasma restored it from a fossil and put a powerful cannon on its back.

KELDEO

Keldeo travels the world visiting beaches and riverbanks, where it can race across the water. When it's determined, it gains blinding speed.

MELOETTA

The Melody Pokémon has a voice that is as beautiful as it is powerful. When singing a duet with the Reveal Glass at the ancient Undersea Temple, it can call forth Landorus, Thundurus, and Tornadus.

Because it has such power and significance, Meloetta is often in danger. It has a special place in its heart for Ash, who has saved it from trouble-with-a-capital-T with Team Rocket on more than one occasion.

Meloetta and Ash first met in Pokéstar Studios in Virbank City. When he spotted some falling equipment, Ash quickly jumped in to save the Mythical Meloetta. From then on, Meloetta began following him around. It even hid in the shadows to cheer for Ash as he battled Gym Leader Roxie for the Toxic Badge. But when Team Rocket stole Meloetta's song and used it at the Abyssal Ruins to summon the Therian Formes of Landorus, Thundurus, and Tornadus, Ash stepped up to help save it and the day.

Ash's Pokémon have a special fondness for Meloetta, too. Oshawott and Piplup are absolutely smitten with the stunning Mythical Pokémon. But no one is closer to Meloetta than its guardian, Ridley, who lives his life to serve and protect it.

VICTINI

Everyone is happy to see the Victory Pokémon because it can turn anyone into a big winner in battle.

DON GEORGE

If you're looking for a practice battle, look no further than the local Pokémon Battle Club. All over Unova, identical cousins and coaches named Don George have set up these special clubhouses where Trainers can come and get matched up for a battle. Ash trained at the Battle Clubs in Accumula Town, Luxuria Town, Nacrene City, Astilbe Town, and Ambiga Town.

Don George also hosts a big regional competition called the Clubsplosion Tournament at the Club Battle Stadium. The winning Trainer is awarded a year's supply of six Pokémon vitamin drinks. Ash, Iris, Cilan, and even Trip tried their luck at this tough competition.

At first glance, muscle-bound Don George might seem like a tough guy, but he's really a big softy when it comes to Pokémon. His love of battles brings tears of joy to his eyes. He isn't just all about training and staying in shape. As Ash discovered, Don George is also full of good advice for Trainers.

TRADE YA!

One of Professor Juniper's technological advancements is the terrific Pokémon Trading Device, which can only be used during battle. Not only does it trade Pokémon to another Trainer, it will also help them evolve.

At Professor Juniper's base camp at Chargestone Cave, she and Bianca decided to use the machine to collect pre-Evolution data and trade Shelmet and Karrablast. In the middle of the battle, with the help of the Pokémon Trading Device, Shelmet evolved into Accelgor, and Karrablast evolved into Escavalier. But the fun wasn't done!

Partly to help Escavalier shed some angry energy, and partly out of excitement to battle with her new Pokémon pal, Professor Juniper immediately suggested they challenge Ash and Cilan together.

The Tag Battle was on: Bianca and Escavalier with Professor Juniper and Accelgor battled Ash and Boldore with Cilan and Crustle. The match was heated, but Crustle's pounding Rock Wrecker left Escavalier and Accelgor unable to battle.

Ash and Cilan won! Bianca was grateful to the professor for all her help, but was still disappointed about losing the battle. Professor Juniper reminded her that earning the trust of her new Pokémon friend during battle was a victory in itself.

BREAKING POKÉMON DISCOVERIES

SYLVEON

FAIRY-TYPES

Researchers have been working tirelessly to gain further knowledge on Pokémon classifications. Through their work, an amazing discovery has just been made: Fairy-type Pokémon! Many Pokémon have even been reclassified as information on this elusive type has come to light. For example, Jigglypuff, Marill, and Gardevoir are now dual-types, with Fairy-type included in their stats.

SWIRLIX

In Kalos alone, you can spot Fairy-types like Flabébé, Spritzee, Swirlix, Sylveon, and even the Legendary Pokémon Xerneas.

The most incredible part of this Pokémon type revelation can be seen on the battlefield. Fairy-type attacks are especially effective on Dragon-types like Noivern, Salamence, and Garchomp.

Still, many questions linger about this mysterious type. It's an important area of study, and many Pokémon scientists are looking to uncover more data on these enchanting and unusual Pokémon.

FLABÉBÉ

XERNEAS

EEVEE AND ITS EVOLUTIONS

Adorable, brown-eyed Eevee is one of a kind. The Evolution Pokémon gets its name from its unique genes. Eevee are easily affected by the radiation found in certain stones that can cause this Pokémon to evolve—or should we say *Eevee*-olve?

Here are all the awesome ways Eevee can change size, shape, and even strength.

VAPOREON

Eevee can evolve into Vaporeon with the aid of a Water Stone. The Bubble Jet Pokémon can turn into a puddle, since its cell composition is close to that of water.

FLAREON

Eevee can evolve into Flareon with the aid of a Fire Stone. Using its flame sac, the Flame Pokémon can instantly turn air into fire.

JOLTEON

Eevee can evolve into Jolteon with the aid of a Thunder Stone. The Lightning Pokémon can fire fierce bolts at its foes.

ESPEON

During daylight, Eevee may evolve into Espeon. The Sun Pokémon can predict the weather with its fur.

UMBREON

In the dark cloak of night, Eevee may evolve into Umbreon. The moon's aura makes its rings glow with a magical strength.

GLACEON

Eevee will only evolve into Glaceon near an Ice Rock. The Fresh Snow Pokémon can make its body temperature drop so low that an icy storm will crush its opponent.

LEAFEON

Eevee will only evolve into Leafeon while in forests containing a Moss Rock. Sunshine powers up this Pokémon through photosynthesis, just like a plant.

SYLVEON

To evolve Eevee into Sylveon, you must teach it a Fairy-type move and give it lots and lots of affection. This Pokémon projects a calming aura from its feelers.

MEGA EVOLUTION

Professor Sycamore of Kalos—more on him on page 144—has been leading the research on a mysterious new form of Evolution. Mega Evolution powers up a Pokémon during battle, causing it to take an entirely new and mighty Mega Evolved form. Unfortunately, not every Pokémon has the ability to Mega Evolve. In fact, even if a Pokémon has a possible Mega Evolved form, its Trainer must still possess three important things to enable his or her Pokémon to Mega Evolve.

BLAZIKEN

First, the bond between the Trainer and their Pokémon must be incredibly tight. They have to completely understand and support each other. Their teamwork and friendship must be as solid as a rock. For example, the Gym Leader of Shalour City, Korrina, insisted she and her best friend, Lucario (more on them on page 153), win a hundred battles straight before they went to Geosenge Town to find Lucarionite—

MEGA BLAZIKEN

GARCHOMP

which brings us to the second thing a Trainer must possess.

Each Pokémon that can possibly Mega Evolve requires a specific Mega Stone to transform. For example, for Garchomp it's Garchompite, for Blaziken it's Blazikenite, for Gardevoir its Gardevoirite, and so on. These rocks are so precious that they cannot be stolen or even taken by an undeserving person. Sorry, Team Rocket, no trap will get you this treasure! And you can't buy a Mega Stone from a merchant like you could with an Evolutionary stone. A Trainer must prove they have what it takes. It's something special a Trainer must quest for.

The third and final piece to unlock Mega Evolution is the Key Stone. Whether placed in a glove, strung on a necklace, set in a band, or even pinned on a necktie, the Trainer must be wearing a Key Stone to help their Pokémon Mega Evolve. This Key Stone links a Trainer to his or her Pokémon in a way that seems almost like a sixth sense. Using a Key Stone, a Trainer can tell how his or her Pokémon feels and see where it is without words.

Once the Key Stone and Mega Stone are shown during a battle, the Pokémon is encased in a cloud of miraculous light. Inside, it temporarily transforms into its Mega Evolved form until it is unable to battle, or until the battle is over. During this period, it is referred to by its name, but with Mega as a prefix—like Mega Blaziken.

MEGA GARCHOMP

POKÉMON	✚	MEGA STONE		MEGA EVOLVED POKÉMON
Abomasnow		Abomasite		Mega Abomasnow
Absol		Absolite		Mega Absol
Aerodactyl		Aerodactylite		Mega Aerodactyl
Aggron		Aggronite		Mega Aggron
Alakazam		Alakazite		Mega Alakazam
Altaria		Altarianite		Mega Altaria
Ampharos		Ampharosite		Mega Ampharos
Audino		Audinite		Mega Audino
Banette		Banettite		Mega Banette
Beedrill		Beedrillite		Mega Beedrill
Blastoise		Blastoisinite		Mega Blastoise
Blaziken		Blazikenite		Mega Blaziken

POKÉMON		MEGA STONE		MEGA EVOLVED POKÉMON
Camerupt 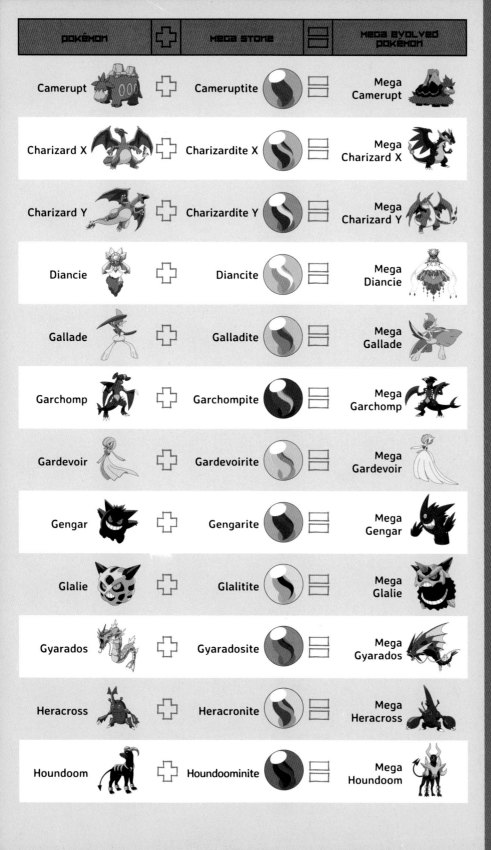		Cameruptite		Mega Camerupt
Charizard X		Charizardite X		Mega Charizard X
Charizard Y		Charizardite Y		Mega Charizard Y
Diancie		Diancite		Mega Diancie
Gallade		Galladite		Mega Gallade
Garchomp		Garchompite		Mega Garchomp
Gardevoir		Gardevoirite		Mega Gardevoir
Gengar		Gengarite		Mega Gengar
Glalie		Glalitite		Mega Glalie
Gyarados		Gyaradosite		Mega Gyarados
Heracross		Heracronite		Mega Heracross
Houndoom		Houndoominite		Mega Houndoom

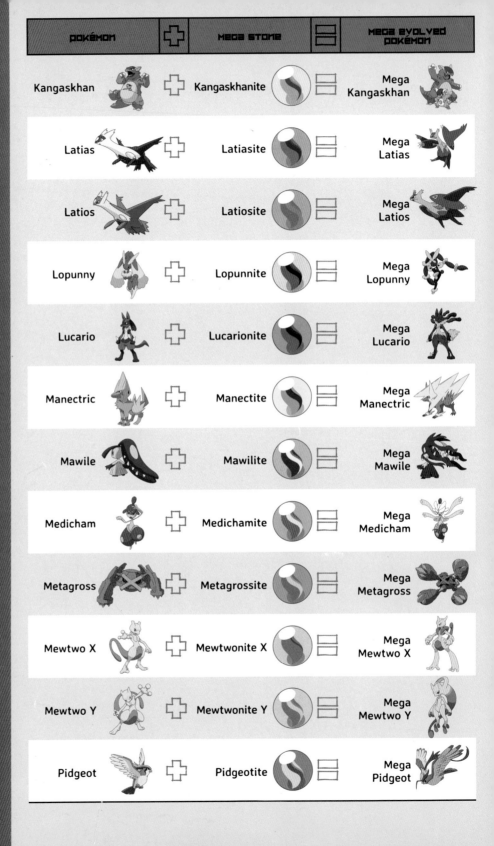

POKÉMON		MEGA STONE		MEGA EVOLVED POKÉMON
Kangaskhan		Kangaskhanite		Mega Kangaskhan
Latias		Latiasite		Mega Latias
Latios		Latiosite		Mega Latios
Lopunny		Lopunnite		Mega Lopunny
Lucario		Lucarionite		Mega Lucario
Manectric		Manectite		Mega Manectric
Mawile		Mawilite		Mega Mawile
Medicham		Medichamite		Mega Medicham
Metagross		Metagrossite		Mega Metagross
Mewtwo X		Mewtwonite X		Mega Mewtwo X
Mewtwo Y		Mewtwonite Y		Mega Mewtwo Y
Pidgeot		Pidgeotite		Mega Pidgeot

POKÉMON		MEGA STONE		MEGA EVOLVED POKÉMON
Pinsir 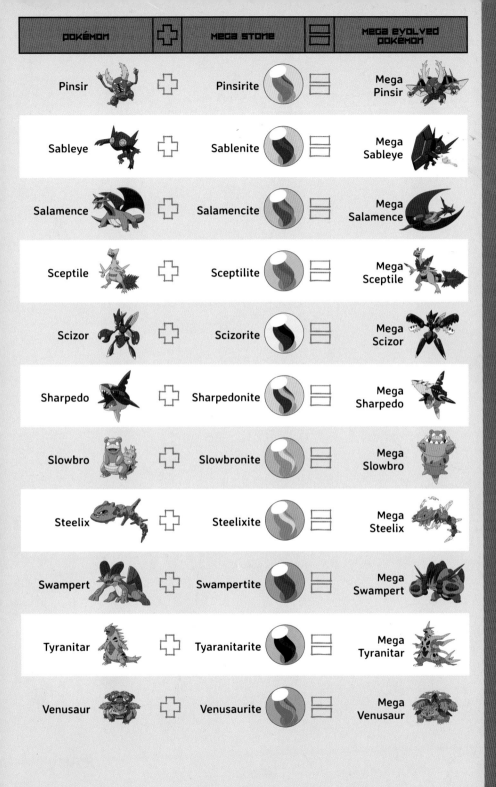	✛	Pinsirite	⊟	Mega Pinsir
Sableye	✛	Sablenite	⊟	Mega Sableye
Salamence	✛	Salamencite	⊟	Mega Salamence
Sceptile	✛	Sceptilite	⊟	Mega Sceptile
Scizor	✛	Scizorite	⊟	Mega Scizor
Sharpedo	✛	Sharpedonite	⊟	Mega Sharpedo
Slowbro	✛	Slowbronite	⊟	Mega Slowbro
Steelix	✛	Steelixite	⊟	Mega Steelix
Swampert	✛	Swampertite	⊟	Mega Swampert
Tyranitar	✛	Tyaranitarite	⊟	Mega Tyranitar
Venusaur	✛	Venusaurite	⊟	Mega Venusaur

KALOS

The gorgeous Kalos region is pure heaven for Pokémon Trainers. Perhaps that's why it's shaped like a star!

Rivers run all through the region, but it's really divided into three main sections: Central, Coastal, and Mountain Kalos—with Lumiose City where they all meet.

If you're an art lover or looking to pick your First Partner Pokémon, then Lumiose City can't be missed. It's to the north, toward the top of the star, and it's a beacon of art and culture. In the center of town is the stunning landmark known as the Prism Tower. It's also home to Professor Sycamore's lab.

THE THREE SUBREGIONS OF KALOS

CENTRAL KALOS

Located to the south of Lumiose City, Central Kalos is like one big botanical garden. The many rivers running through it feed the lush greenery. So instead of traveling on foot, you can bring a paddle and boat and row your way between towns. Two popular destinations in Central Kalos are Santalune City and entitled Princess Allie's home, the Parfum Palace.

COASTAL KALOS

A vast ocean borders the western part of the region. Rocky cliffs line the coast. To the northwest, the shore is dotted with giant rocks and boulders. Even more stones can be found among the merchants of Geosenge Town. And a stone more powerful still resides in the Tower of Mastery in Shalour City.

A note to travelers: Beware of the crystals in Reflection Cave. It's tempting to check yourself out in a mirror, but you just might find yourself face-to-face with your exact opposite.

MOUNTAIN KALOS

To the east is a cool part of Kalos known for its colder temperatures. If you're easily spooked, avoid the marshes to the northeast. They're rumored to be haunted. But if you're a fan of any sport that requires snow, don't miss the chance to check out this subregion!

KALOS FIRST PARTNER POKÉMON

CHESPIN

If fun-loving Chespin had a middle name, it just might be trouble. This curious Pokémon is always poking around looking for adventure. On and off the battlefield, the Spiny Nut Pokémon is sure to be where the action is.

CHESPIN EVOLVES INTO QUILLADIN, THEN CHESNAUGHT.

FENNEKIN

Fennekin's ears are always burning—even when no one is talking about it. The Fox Pokémon has fluffy fur inside its ears that can fire up a battle with 390°F. And if a stranger gets in its way, it has a hot temper to match. Fennekin fuels this flaming fluff by snacking on twigs.

FENNEKIN EVOLVES INTO BRAIXEN, THEN DELPHOX.

FROAKIE

Don't let Froakie's big eyes fool you into thinking it's just staring off into space. It's one smart Pokémon. The Bubble Frog Pokémon can also jump high to dodge attacks, or even stick it to its opponents by throwing the gummy bubbles on its back.

FROAKIE EVOLVES INTO FROGADIER, THEN GRENINJA.

PROFESSOR SYCAMORE

The lanky professor with a mop of black hair is the leading Pokémon researcher in Kalos. Sycamore focuses his studies on Pokémon Evolution—he's the foremost authority on a new phenomenon known as Mega Evolution. More on that on page 134!

At his lab in Lumiose City, Sycamore has a spectacular Pokémon habitat perfect for his research and for playing around. Along with his pal Garchomp and his lab assistants, they care for hundreds of Pokémon friends. But when the weather turns warm, you can find Professor Sycamore at his annual summer camp for Trainers.

CLEMONT

Clemont met Ash in his hometown—when a robot ejected Ash from the Gym for not having enough badges. When Ash went flying, Clemont immediately opened up a portable, inflatable giant pillow to break his fall. Ash was grateful to the friendly stranger. He had no idea Clemont was actually the Gym Leader of Lumiose City.

While Clemont is shy about admitting he's the keeper of the Voltage Badge, it's hard for him to keep his intelligence a secret! Clemont's always happy to have his scientific projects and imperfect inventions save the day. It's amazing what wonderful gadgets he's got in that little backpack. Since he's such a technological whiz, it comes as no surprise that he's an Electric-type expert. But it might surprise you to learn that he's also an excellent chef.

Clemont was inspired to join Ash on his journey after watching him bravely save Garchomp—more on that on page 148! He left his Clembot robot behind to take his place as Gym Leader.

CLEMONT'S POKÉMON

CHESPIN   BUNNELBY   LUXIO

BONNIE

Clemont's kid sister might as well be his shadow. She follows him everywhere, hoping for the chance to help him with his Pokémon friends. She's obsessed, especially with the adorable Dedenne that she carries in her purse.

Bonnie isn't quite old enough to be a Trainer, so she relishes the experiences Clemont shares with her. She is thrilled about joining him and Ash on the road, with her dad's, blessing, of course. Clemont is a sweet older brother who's always looking out for this enthusiastic little girl.

MEYER

This impressive superhero keeps saving Ash just in the nick of time—from a fall at the Prism Tower to a run-in with Mega-Mega-Meowth. At first, Ash's savior's identity was a mystery, until Clemont and Bonnie introduced him as Meyer, their dad.

Backed by his Pokémon Blaziken and Ampharos, Meyer is very tough and brave. But when it comes to his kids, he's made of mush. He sheds happy tears when Clemont and Bonnie tell him about their desire to travel with their new friend, Ash. He's one proud papa!

FROAKIE

The first Pokémon Ash caught in Kalos was Froakie. He'd been warned that this Pokémon was a handful that'd been returned by more than one Trainer—more on that on the next page. But Ash was happy to begin his travels in Kalos with the Bubble Frog Pokémon by his side. Froakie has proven to be a loyal friend. With Ash as its Trainer, it has only increased its strength and speed.

HAWLUCHA

Heroic Hawlucha is called the Forest Champion because it always stands up for the little guy. Ash met Hawlucha when it was locked in battle with an Ursaring who'd been scaring three smaller Pokémon and stealing their berries. Impressed with Hawlucha's swagger, Ash helped the Wrestling Pokémon incorporate its signature pose into its battle strategy. Hawlucha wanted to learn everything it could from its new friend Ash, and it asked to join him on his journey.

FLETCHLING

Although Ash met Fletchling when it stole a Berry from Dedenne, he decided it was a Pokémon he could use on his team. Ash called on Froakie to help him catch his second Pokémon in Kalos. The battle relied heavily on Froakie's jumping ability to hop from cliff to ledge to follow the Normal-Flying-type, but it proved to be a successful strategy. In the end, it was well worth the effort to catch Ash's feisty friend, the Tiny Robin Pokémon.

HOW ASH MET FROAKIE

The first Pokémon Ash caught in Kalos was Froakie. Although it seemed more like Froakie caught Ash than the other way around!

The Trainer and the Bubble Frog Pokémon met on Ash's very first day in the Kalos region. After being ejected from the Lumiose City Gym, Ash was hungry for a fun battle. So he and his new friend, Clemont, decided to practice with Bunnelby and Pikachu.

Unfortunately, as the battle wore on, they ran into some real challengers—Team Rocket. They'd followed Ash all the way to Kalos, and they had only one thing on their mind: stealing Pikachu!

"*Piiiikachuuuuu!*" Pikachu yelped as it fired off a terrific Thunderbolt.

"Wobbuffet, use Mirror Coat," Jessie cried.

Following orders, Wobbuffet created a rainbow-like sheen over its body that bounced the attack back at Pikachu with twice as much strength.

"Pikachu!" Ash cried. "Are you okay?"

Pikachu nodded, ready to keep fighting.

"Ash, we'd better retreat," Clemont begged. "There's no way we can beat Mirror Coat."

"I've never run, and I'm not going to start now," Ash declared. "If we don't stand up to Team Rocket, who will?!"

So Clemont had Bunnelby try Mud Shot. While Wobbuffet was distracted dodging the dirt balls, Pikachu tried to slip in an Electro Ball. But Wobbuffet quickly used Mirror Coat to deflect it.

Pikachu was about to get another whopping taste of its own electric power when suddenly a stranger appeared to save it! Froakie leaped out of a nearby tree and grabbed Pikachu.

"Froakie froak froooakie!" Froakie hurled its gummy frubbles at Team Rocket.

Wobbuffet's Mirror Coat couldn't stop those globs of gunk, because they weren't an attack. So Team Rocket was stuck—literally! The sticky goop had them glued in place.

"Way to go, Froakie!" Ash cheered.

Clemont had Bunnelby use Dig to sneak up on Team Rocket. Then Pikachu used Thunderbolt, and Froakie added a powerful pulse to blast off Jessie, James, Meowth, and Wobbuffet!

Unfortunately, Team Rocket landed in a tree right across from Professor Sycamore's lab. So when Ash rushed Froakie there to recharge, Team Rocket saw the perfect chance to plot their revenge.

Inside the lab, Professor Sycamore was very relieved to see his old friend Froakie. He immediately had his assistant, Sophie, take Froakie in for treatment. Then he explained to Ash that the first partner Pokémon had been let go by its Trainer and had gone missing.

"Who would abandon that awesome Froakie?!" Ash wondered.

Professor Sycamore explained that Froakie had a history of being returned by Trainers. It seemed no one could handle the headstrong Pokémon.

Just then, one of Professor Sycamore's Pokémon pals—a giant Garchomp—stopped by to visit. It was worried about its friend Froakie.

"Don't worry, Froakie will be just fine in no time!" Professor Sycamore promised it. "And we have Ash and his friends to thank for that."

Garchomp was so grateful to Ash that it let all the kids pet it—even little Bonnie.

While Froakie was resting, Professor Sycamore offered to show Ash and his friends around his lab. It was home to many Pokémon who helped the professor with his research. Professor Sycamore had a whole habitat growing under a glass roof.

Unfortunately, that glass roof proved to be the perfect way for Team Rocket to eavesdrop.

Once they heard about these special Pokémon that Professor Sycamore was raising, they couldn't wait to steal one!

A few minutes later, there was a knock at the lab door. When Sophie opened it, she found Team Rocket dressed up in lab coats, pretending to be Mega Evolution experts.

Their disguises didn't fool Froakie for a minute! *"Froak froakie!"* it warned Garchomp.

Before the Pokémon could take action, James tossed out a mysterious collar. Garchomp jumped in front of Froakie to protect its pal, and the collar locked around its neck.

"Gaaaaarchooomp!" it screamed.

Filled with rage, Garchomp blasted Team Rocket out of the lab, but it was too late. The collar had a hold on Garchomp, and turned it into a fighting machine! Using Hyper Beam, Garchomp blasted its way out of the lab and stormed down the street on a rampage.

"Oh, no! What's got into Garchomp?! We've got to get that collar off!" Ash cried, rallying Pikachu and Froakie to go after the angry Pokémon.

"People of Lumiose City, please stay inside. There is an angry Garchomp on the loose," Officer Jenny warned over the loudspeaker.

Garchomp headed to the Prism Tower and climbed up the side. Then it began firing Hyper Beam blasts from the sky.

Ash knew he had to get up the tower to Garchomp—but how?

"I've got the perfect invention for this situation in my backpack!" Clemont promised. Using a silver prong, he popped open the door to the Prism Tower's emergency staircase.

"Wow!" Ash said, impressed.

Ash, Pikachu, and Froakie raced up the stairs to get to Garchomp. But Garchomp was less than thrilled to see them.

"Garchooooooomp!" it yelped, firing a Hyper Beam directly at them.

Pikachu went to counterattack with Thunderbolt, but Ash stopped him. After all, it was

their friend Garchomp!
He wanted to try to
reason with it.

"*Gaaaarrrrchomp!*" it
screamed, trying to pull the
collar off.

But the collar wouldn't
budge, no matter how hard
the Mach Pokémon yanked at it.
Garchomp was struggling so much that it lost
its balance and was about to fall off the ledge!

Quick-thinking Froakie tossed its gummy frubbles at Garchomp's feet so it couldn't fall. Once it was stuck in place, Ash came up with a plan.

"Pikachu, use Iron Tail to cut off the collar," Ash asked.

"*Pikachuuuuuu!*" the Electric-type cried, slicing through that horrible device around Garchomp's neck.

Success! But Pikachu's Iron Tail was so strong, the Prism Tower started to crumble—and Pikachu slipped with the rubble.

"Pikachu!" Ash screamed, diving off the edge to save his best friend.

Out of the blue, a strong Pokémon swooped in and saved them. It looked like a big fiery comet flying through the night sky. Ash didn't get a chance to thank the heroic Pokémon—it was gone in a flash. But he learned later it was a Mega Evolved Blaziken.

Back at the lab, Professor Sycamore and Garchomp thanked Ash and Pikachu for all their help.

"Don't forget Froakie!" Ash added.

"*Froakie,*" it said, blushing.

Professor Sycamore gave Ash a special Kalos region Pokédex. Ash was so grateful for the gift, but there was an even bigger one waiting for him at the lab's gate—friendship!

Before Ash left, Froakie placed a Poké Ball in front of him. "*Froaaakie?*" it asked Ash.

"Really, buddy, you choose me?" Ash cheered.

Froakie nodded.

"*Pikachu!*" Ash's best pal cheered.

So Ash tossed the Poké Ball and officially caught his first Pokémon pal in Kalos.

SERENA

Most faces in Kalos are new to Ash, but he and Serena go way back. They both went to Professor Oak's summer camp. She remembers Ash fondly as the boy who wrapped his handkerchief around her wounded knee. When camp ended, they went their separate ways, and Serena returned home to Kalos, taking the memories and handkerchief with her.

Since her camp days, Serena had been studying with her mother, a decorated Rhyhorn racer. However, she just couldn't seem to get Rhyhorn to do anything but toss her off.

So, when she saw Ash on television saving Garchomp at Prism Tower, she decided she had to find him. Her first stop was with Professor Sycamore. At his lab in Lumiose City, she picked up her first partner Pokémon, Fennekin, and asked for information about where Ash was headed . . . to a whole other town!

When she finally caught up with Ash in Santalune City, he was in the middle of battling Gym Leader Viola for the Bug Badge. He insulted Serena by forgetting who she was.

But Serena didn't let that bother her. She gave Ash the advice he'd shared with her so many years ago: "Don't give up until it's over." With her support, he turned the battle around and won! Serena has been a trusted friend ever since. She's constantly whipping up fun—and cookies, like delicious macaroons and Poké Puffs.

On the road, Serena seemed to lose her way—and her goal of becoming a Rhyhorn racer. Ash helped her get back on track and find her true passion— becoming a Pokémon performer who competes in Pokémon Showcases.

PANCHAM

KORRINA

The unassuming girl who glides around on heart-decorated skates with a matching helmet is actually the Gym Leader of Shalour City. Korrina is practically nobility when it comes to Mega Evolution. Her family tree is filled with Gym Leaders who've trained Lucario that can Mega Evolve. In fact, it's said that her grandfather Gurkinn is a direct descendent of the Trainer who first created a Mega Evolution. So, ever since she was a little girl, that's always been her dream.

DIANTHA

The Champion of the Kalos region has a Mega Evolving Gardevoir and a major sweet tooth! But she's best known for being a famous movie star. Ash first met this beautiful icon right before a big televised battle. Although Ash was bummed he couldn't challenge her right then and there, she promised to battle him once he beat the Kalos League—that is, if her publicist Kathie Lee lets anyone get a minute with her. Even charming Professor Sycamore has a hard time sweet-talking his way into the chance to study the celebrity and her Gardevoir.

LEGENDARY POKÉMON OF KALOS

XERNEAS

Even more spectacular than the spectrum of color on its rainbow horns is the Fairy-type's incredible gift. According to legend, the Life Pokémon can grant immortality.

YVELTAL

Don't get too close to the dark Destruction Pokémon. It can absorb another's life energy.

ZYGARDE

In times of great chaos in Kalos, this Legendary Pokémon will reveal itself and restore order. And that power is precisely where it gets its name—the Order Pokémon.

MYTHICAL POKEMON OF KALOS

DIANCIE

Using only its hands, Diancie can compress carbon from the atmosphere into diamonds. According to myths, when Carbink transforms into Diancie, it is an unbelievably dazzling sight.

VOLCANION

This Pokémon Volcanion lives in the mountains and stays far away from humans. The arms on its back can shoot out steam with incredibly destructive force, though it often uses these steam clouds to cover its escape.

HOOPA

According to myth, Hoopa can summon whatever it wants with the enormous power of its six rings. When that power is confined, it is much smaller and less destructive.

ALOLA

Alola is made up of four islands: Melemele, Akala, Poni, and Ula'ula. There are many native Pokémon that have existed in Alola for generations as well as Pokémon that have come to the island paradise from other regions.

Ash starts his Alolan adventure right on Melemele Island. Some lucky students get to attend the local Pokémon School on the shore. Now those are classrooms with a view!

Akala Island is home to the Wela Volcano. Ash first visits the island when he helps his buddy Kiawe deliver Moomoo Milk from his family's farm on Akala.

RIDE POKÉMON

Traveling around Alola can be fun in a car, boat, or even on foot, but nothing tops a tour from a Pokémon pal! Known as Ride Pokémon, these awesome drivers will steer you through to the destination of your choice. A Ride Pokémon might even be your partner in a race! But fast or slow, it's always a blast when you can hop on someone else's back.

Speed through the sea with Sharpedo! Ash was able to not only ride the waves, but explore around underwater on a Ride Sharpedo trip.

Gallop across the grove with Tauros! At the Pokémon School, students hold rallies with Ride Tauros. Race you to class!

Soar above the clouds with a Ride Pelipper! Ash was amazed at how fast a Ride Pelipper could fly.

ROWLET

During the day, Rowlet rests and generates energy via photosynthesis. In the night, it flies silently to sneak up on foes and launch a flurry of kicking attacks.

ROWLET EVOLVES INTO DARTRIX, THEN DECIDUEYE.

LITTEN

When it grooms its fur, Litten is storing up ammunition— the flaming fur is later coughed up in a fiery attack. Trainers often have a hard time getting this solitary Pokémon to trust them.

LITTEN EVOLVES INTO TORRACAT, THEN INCINEROAR.

POPPLIO

Popplio uses the water balloons it blows from its nose as a weapon in battle. It's a hard worker and puts in lots of practice creating and controlling these balloons.

POPPLIO EVOLVES INTO BRIONNE, THEN PRIMARINA.

PRINCIPAL SAMSON OAK

When Ash first meets Samson Oak, he thinks he's found a familiar face in Alola, but he's really just a relative of one. Samson Oak is the cousin of the famous Professor Oak of Kanto and he is the principal of the Pokémon School.

The resemblance between the two cousins goes way beyond looks. Samson Oak shares a love of science and Pokémon with his cousin. Samson Oak's area of research is regional variants of Pokémon, such as Alolan Exeggutor.

For someone who studies something so serious, Samson Oak is a really easygoing guy with a silly sense of humor. The principal can't resist making puns out of Pokémon names—what about *'chu*?

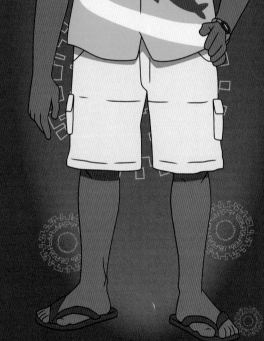

KOMALA

Principal Samson Oak's best Pokémon pal is Komala.

Komala never wakes up—ever—although it does sometimes move around as it dreams. It lives in a permanent state of sleep, cuddling its precious log or its Trainer's arm.

PROFESSOR KUKUI

Professor Kukui is a favorite teacher among the students at the Pokémon School. He invited Ash to stay at his home in Alola so that he could attend the special school.

Professor Kukui's area of expertise is Pokémon moves—he likes to sneak Pokémon attack names into his everyday conversations. You won't find this sporty schoolteacher spending all his time inside a lab. Professor Kukui loves to get hands-on experience in the great outdoors.

Professor Kukui's dream is to someday start a Pokémon League in Alola. In the meantime, he practices his battle techniques as the Masked Royal, a mysterious and mighty television star whose true identity is secret.

PROFESSOR BURNET

Professor Kukui's partner is a highly respected and renowned researcher. Professor Burnet focuses her studies on Ultra Wormholes, the path by which Ultra Beasts leave their world. In addition to being a scientist, Professor Burnet is also an incredible inventor. At the Aether Foundation, she has created numerous pieces of technology. But this well-loved professor doesn't like to just sit in the lab—she is always there to lend a hand and keep Ash and his friends informed. Between her brains and her charisma, it is no wonder she received the Alola Woman of the Year Award.

ASH'S POKÉMON IN ALOLA

ROWLET

Ash happily shared his lunch with a hungry wild Rowlet, then followed it to meet its Pikipek pals. They arrived just as Team Rocket was trying to catch the Pikipek in their net! Ash and Pikachu snapped into action and battled Team Rocket so Rowlet had a chance to free its friends. After that, Rowlet wouldn't let Ash go anywhere until he offered to take it along, too!

ROCKRUFF ⇨ DUSK FORM LYCANROC

After Ash helped a wild Rockruff learn Rock Throw for its rematch with Magmar, they both realized they were meant to train together! So, Rockruff joined Ash on his journey and never lost its fighting spirit. It jumped at the chance to help Ash win his grand trial with Kahuna Olivia. Soon after the heated match, it caught the attention of the Island Guardian of Akala, Tapu Lele, who helped Rockruff evolve during a stunning sunset into a rare Lycanroc Dusk Form. Read more about its evolution on page 170.

LITTEN ⇨ TORRACAT

When Ash offered a hungry wild Litten some of his sandwich, it helped itself to an even bigger bite. At first, Ash was annoyed, but when he realized Litten had been feeding an old Stoutland, he vowed to come to its aid. After battling back Litten's bullies—Alolan Persian and Team Rocket—Ash got his chance to catch his new Pokémon pal, but he still had to earn its trust. In time, they became an awesome team and took on the famous Masked Royal, twice. During the rematch, Litten was so fired up it evolved into Torracat.

KIAWE

Some people take a bus to school, but Kiawe has a much cooler ride—his best buddy, Charizard. They do everything together, including delivering milk from his family's farm.

Kiawe didn't catch Charizard—the Flame Pokémon was passed down from his grandfather. But Kiawe isn't the kind of guy who easily accepts gifts or help. He is headstrong and proud, which can sometimes make him seem grumpy. He works hard for what he has—and that includes the Z-Ring given to him by Kahuna Olivia of Akala Island.

KIAWE'S POKÉMON

CHARIZARD

Charizard seeks out stronger foes and only breathes fire during battles with worthy opponents. The fiery breath is so hot that it can melt any material.

TURTONATOR

Poisonous gases and flames spew from Turtonator's nostrils. Its shell is made of unstable material that might explode upon impact, so opponents are advised to aim for its stomach instead.

ALOLAN MAROWAK

The flaming bone that Marowak spins like a baton once belonged to its mother, and it's protected by its mother's spirit. It grieves for its fallen companions, and visits their graves along the roadside.

LANA

Lana is one of Ash's classmates, but she's not the kind of student who's always raising her hand. Lana struggles to find words to express what she's thinking and feeling, but she's by no means a pushover. In fact, Lana can be quite stubborn, and she likes to get her own way. This can be a challenge since Lana lives with her grandmother, parents, twin younger sisters, and a bunch of fishermen. Even if Lana wanted to talk, how would she ever get a word in edgewise?

POPPLIO

Popplio uses the water balloons it blows from its nose as a weapon in battle. It's a hard worker and puts in lots of practice creating and controlling these balloons.

When Ash's class went on a fishing trip, Professor Kukui put Lana in charge. Everyone was surprised when Team Rocket showed up and scooped up all their Pokémon in a net. Then Team Rocket dropped the Pokémon toward some rocks! Fortunately, Lana's Popplio quickly created a giant water balloon to cushion the fall and save the day!

MALLOW

Mallow is a ball of energy! She runs on instinct and isn't afraid to dive into any situation, but she occasionally jumps to conclusions. In fact, Mallow loves all kinds of jumping—both in her mind and on the field. One of her favorite things to do is play sports. She's also a very good cook and often helps out at the local restaurant, where she lives with her brother and father.

Mallow has a lot to give, and she never gives up. She is very protective of her good friends Lana and Lillie. When she cares about something, she gives it her all.

MALLOW'S POKÉMON

 ➡

BOUNSWEET

Bounsweet smells good enough to eat—which sometimes gets it into trouble! The intensely sugary liquid it gives off can be diluted to bring the sweetness level down so people can drink it.

STEENEE

Lively and cheerful, Steenee often attracts a crowd of other Pokémon drawn to its energy and its lovely scent. Its sepals have evolved into a hard shell to protect its head and body from attackers.

SOPHOCLES

Sophocles acts like a slacker, but he's actually really motivated to learn about technology. A computer programming whiz, he's obsessed with how the Rotom Pokédex works and has even taken one apart to get a closer look.

Sophocles can explain even the most complex things about tech, but otherwise, he might come off as a nervous wreck. He is a sensitive soul who relates better to machines than he does to people.

SOPHOCLES'S POKÉMON

TOGEDEMARU

Its back is covered with long, spiny fur that usually lies flat. Togedemaru can bristle up the fur during battle for use as a weapon, or during storms to attract lightning, which it stores as electricity in its body.

CHARJABUG

When Charjabug breaks down food for energy, some of that energy is stored as electricity inside its body. A Trainer who likes to go camping would appreciate having this Pokémon as a partner!

LILLIE

Lillie's family is wealthy—her butler drives her to school every day! Some might think she's a total snob, but, in fact, Lillie is one of the kindest kids at the Pokémon School. And she's also one of the hardest-working students.

Lillie wants to learn all she can about Pokémon . . . but would you believe that for a long time, she didn't like touching them? Fortunately, all that changed once she met her best Pokémon buddy, Alolan Vulpix.

ALOLAN VULPIX

Vulpix in the Alola region were once known as Keokeo, and some older folks still use that name. Its six tails can create a spray of ice crystals to cool itself off when it gets too hot.

When Principal Oak tasked Ash's class with taking care of a Pokémon Egg, someone had to volunteer to bring it home with them after school. To help Lillie get over her fear of touching Pokémon, Mallow suggested she be responsible for the Egg. At first, Lillie was nervous. But when a hungry Salandit went after the Egg, she threw her arms around the Egg to protect it. It later hatched and revealed an Alolan Vulpix!

Professor Kukui has been teaching Ash all about what makes for an amazing Z-Move. First, a Trainer needs a Z-Ring, a band made of square metal plates. In the center of the Z-ring lies a large plate that holds the Z-Crystal. But this key tool isn't all a Trainer needs to use a Z-move.

The Z-Crystal and Z-Ring are powered by heart. A Pokémon and its Trainer must share a bond so strong that the Z-Ring can transform their feelings into power. However, their battle goals cannot be selfish. They must be fighting for something bigger than themselves—like helping the islands, helping Pokémon, or helping others. Only those who truly care about all living things in our world are permitted to use Z-Moves.

Kiawe earned his Z-Ring in a ceremony called the Island Challenge. Ash's first Z-Ring was a present from the guardian of Melemele Island, Tapu Koko. He earned his second Z-Crystal after completing an Island Challenge under the watchful eye of the island kahuna, Hala.

THE ISLAND KAHUNA

Every island in Alola has its own kahuna. In order to participate in the Island Challenge, Trainers need to seek the permission of the island kahuna. If the island kahuna decides that the Pokémon Trainer is worthy enough, it will assign a trial for the Trainer to complete. Only the island kahuna can decide if the Trainer has passed or failed the trial challenge.

If a Trainer proves him or herself and passes the first trial, the next step is the island's grand trial—battling the big kahuna himself.

THE ISLAND CHALLENGE

The Island Challenge is the kind of trial that tests a Trainer and teaches him or her skills to be stronger in battle. The kahuna of Melemele Island, Hala, explained to Ash that the challenge's true purpose is to give young people an appreciation for Alola's natural wonder. A Trainer wins the challenge when he or she recognizes how important it is to protect the islands on behalf of the many people and Pokémon who call Alola home.

For his first trial, Ash battled Totem Gumshoos to gain its help in chasing Rattata and Raticate away. Then, Ash earned the chance to battle the kahuna Hala, in the grand trial—and he won!

Ash's second Island Challenge was not as straightforward. Olivia was preparing her famous Akala Curry, and to help her gather the special ingredient, Ash and Litten battled Totem Lurantis. Using the bold Z-Move Breakneck Blitz, Ash was able snag the Revival Herbs for Olivia's recipe and a Grass-type Z-Crystal. And he passed his initial trial for the Island Challenge!

At his grand trial with Kahuna Olivia, Ash and his pals Rowlet and Rockruff faced Probopass and Lycanroc, the evolved form of Rockruff. But with awesome energy and a clever strategy, Ash won the match!

HOW ROCKRUFF EVOLVED

It was in the wee hours of the night after Ash won his second grand trial against the kahuna of Akala, Olivia. And what a day it had been! The battle was intense, but with the help of Rowlet and Rockruff, Ash was awarded a Rock-type Z-Crystal. Most of his Pokémon partners were sound asleep after their big battle, but one was still wide awake. Every time Rockruff closed its eyes, it was haunted by a mistake it had made earlier that kept replaying in its head.

All day, Rockruff had been ready for battle. It was snarling and strutting. It was so raring to go, it thought Ash had called its name to battle when he started to say a name beginning with "R"—though Ash was saying "Rowlet." But Rockruff's enthusiasm convinced Ash to choose it next.

Rockruff was ready to give the grand trial its all! It fired rounds of tough Rock Throw moves and pounced on Lycanroc with Bite. When Probopass aimed a Zap Cannon blast right at Rowlet, Rockruff was quick on its feet and stopped it with one of Probopass's own Mini Noses. And it was Rockruff who sealed the win with a smart move—it climbed Lycanroc's Rock Slide to deliver a close range Rock Throw.

But that's not what Rockruff was up thinking about. Even after all those battle moments it was proud of, the Puppy Pokémon couldn't help but feel embarrassed by one blunder. In the heat of the moment, it got too excited, lost sight of what was happening—and Rockruff attacked its own friend and battle buddy, Rowlet.

When Rowlet had followed Ash's instructions and tried to fly Rockruff up off the battlefield and into the sky again, Rockruff lashed out and whacked Rowlet with its tail. In that single, strong swipe, Rowlet was knocked out.

"*Arrrrrr arrr,*" Rockruff whimpered during the battle, seeing its pal Rowlet in Ash's arms with its eyes closed.

Rockruff immediately walked over to apologize. Ash knew it hadn't meant any harm, and he got down on all fours and told Rockruff that they were in this battle together! Then, together, they won the match.

But winning wasn't everything, especially when you felt like you hurt someone you cared about.

Now, while Rockruff's pals Ash, Litten, Pikachu, and Rowlet were sleeping soundly, Rockruff sneaked out of the house. It needed to blow off some steam, so it headed for the forest.

"*Rrrr rrrrr,*" Rockruff growled, firing a Rock Throw at the mountainside.

As falling rocks hailed down from the mountain, Rockruff raced around to dodge them. The Puppy Pokémon thought it was alone, but it had caught the attention of one of Akala's most famous inhabitants—Tapu Lele, the Island Guardian.

Playful Tapu Lele giggled watching Rockruff challenge itself. It wanted in on the action! So, Tapu Lele swooped down and sealed the area in a glowing pink Psychic Terrain. Rockruff was trapped inside the battlefield bubble, but it was ready!

"*Rrrrrr!*" Rowlet roared, lunging at Tapu Lele.

But it quickly got knocked back down to the ground. Then Tapu Lele, bathed in a ball of sparkling light, swooped down and slammed right into Rockruff.

"*Arrrr arrrr,*" Rockruff whimpered, struggling to get back up on its four feet. But the minute it did, Tapu Lele continued to strike it with strong smacks.

Luckily, backup was on the way!

Ash and Pikachu were coming through the forest, searching for their Puppy Pokémon pal.

"Rockruff!" Ash called out into the

darkness of the woods. "Where are you?"

"*Pikachu!*" Pikachu shouted.

Tapu Lele was within earshot of the pair, and decided to disappear before they spotted it. The pink battle bubble and the Island Guardian were gone in a flash!

Soon, Ash and Pikachu found their friend. Rockruff was lying on the ground, looking like it was in rough shape. Ash tried to pick up his pal, but Rockruff jumped up on its feet and growled.

"You've got to get to a Pokémon Center now!" Ash said. "You need help from Nurse Joy."

But Rockruff just howled and ran away. So Ash chased after the Puppy Pokémon and scooped it up in his arms.

"*Rrrrrr!*" Rockruff replied, sinking its teeth into Ash's arm.

Then Rockruff realized that it had done it again. It bit a friend. It was so embarrassed, it rushed into the bushes to hide.

The next morning, when Ash, Pikachu, and Rockruff were missing, all their friends were worried. Mallow, Steenee, Lana, Popplio, Kiawe, Litten, Rowlet, Rotom Dex, Togedemaru, Lillie, Snowy, Sophocles, Professor Kukui, and even Kahuna Olivia and Lycanroc searched the area looking for their pals.

"I checked all over Paniola Town, but no luck," Kiawe said.

"Where could they have gotten off to?" Sophocles wondered.

Just then, Ash and Pikachu walked up. They were exhausted, and they knew they were in trouble.

"Wandering off in the middle of the night is inexcusable!" Professor Kukui said.

"I'm sorry," Ash replied. "Rockruff disappeared, so I went after it. I was really worried."

Ash told his friends that when he found Rockruff, it ran away. Kahuna Olivia thought Rockruff might be behaving strangely because it was about to go through a big change.

"Lycanroc suddenly disappeared on me just before it evolved," Olivia shared. "It finally came back, but only after its Evolution was complete."

Ash hoped Olivia was right, but he and his pals weren't going to give up their search. Kiawe climbed on Charizard to search in the sky. Lana and Popplio, Mallow and Steenee, and Lillie and Snowy headed out on foot. Sophocles started researching possible scenarios. Even Olivia's buddy, Lycanroc Midday Form, headed out on a search mission. Ash was so grateful to his friends!

Up on the mountain, a very tired Rockruff was roaming around. It cried out with a loud howl.

Another trainer named Gladion and his Pokémon pal Lycanroc Midnight Form were close by. Lycanroc could not resist the call of Rockruff, and took off to find it. Now two Lycanroc were searching for Rockruff!

Meanwhile, Rockruff continued to climb the narrow mountain pass. Suddenly, a squawking Fearow startled it. Rockruff slipped off the ledge—and fell all the way down into the river.

"Arrrrroooooo!" Rockruff yelped.

When the two Lycanroc followed the sound, they finally found Rockruff, who was wet and whimpering. They carried it back to the Ruins of Life, where the epic battle with Olivia had taken place. It was a shrine to Tapu Lele, and the Island Guardian itself was there, sprinkling its magical, healing scales.

"Tapu lele lele tapu!" it sang as it fluttered about.

The Lycanroc lay Rockruff down on the stone battlefield. Lycanroc Midnight Form called out to Tapu Lele and asked for help, but Tapu Lele sent it flying into the mountainside.

"Lycan," Lycanroc Midnight Form whispered.

Then Lycanroc Midday Form bravely asked Tapu Lele again to help Rockruff. Suddenly, the Island Guardian looked down at the poor Puppy Pokémon and realized it was the same one it had battled the night before.

"*Tapu-u-u-u-u lele,*" it giggled as it scattered its scales, restoring Rockruff's strength.

But then, Tapu Lele's mood suddenly changed. It sent Lycanroc Midday flying at the mountainside, too.

Nearby, Ash, Pikachu, Rotom Dex, Litten, Professor Kiawe, and Kahuna Olivia spotted some sparkles.

"*Pika pika!*" Pikachu signaled, knowing Tapu Lele and Rockruff must be close.

"That isn't good," Olivia said. "Tapu Lele thinks it's being playful, when in fact it's being cruel. It's so strong, it doesn't realize it could leave its opponent badly injured during one of its playful battles!"

Ash didn't need to hear any more. He raced off in the direction of the sparkles. He ran uphill through the woods, pushing through the shrubs and climbing up the mountainside, until he arrived at the Ruins of Life. There, he was relieved to find his Puppy Pokémon pal, Rockruff. But Ash also saw the Lycanroc facing off with Tapu Lele.

"No, don't!" Ash begged Tapu Lele, putting himself in harm's way to cover his Pokémon pals.

As the rest of Ash's crew arrived, they saw Tapu Lele sneakily sapping the energy of Ash and Lycanroc. Rings of rainbow light surrounded the four of them on the battlefield.

"Of course! That's Draining Kiss," Professor Kukui explained. "Tapu Lele is taking the energy it drains from Ash and both Lycanroc and then giving it to Rockruff!"

Rockruff opened its eyes and saw its pal Ash. It licked Ash's face until he woke up, too.

"Rockruff, you're all right!" Ash cheered.

Tapu Lele soared off toward the sun, pleased with what it had done. Rockruff walked to the edge of the ruins and stared out at the sunset, which was glowing green.

"Wow, check out that sun!" Ash said.

Suddenly, Rockruff's eyes and entire body glowed green to match the green sun.

It evolved into a rare form of Lycanroc—Dusk Form.

"The fact that it evolved this way must be a result of the green flash!" Professor Kukui said.

"Wow! What's the green flash?" Ash asked.

"It's when the sun's light is green for an instant at sunset," Professor Kukui replied.

"The green flash is something that is hardly ever seen," Olivia added. "Legend says those who have witnessed the green flash are given a bit of extraordinarily good luck!"

Ash already felt extraordinarily lucky to have a friend in Lycanroc Dusk Form. He and his friends from the Pokémon School said good-bye to the kahuna of Akala Island. They headed back to Melemele Island together, in search of more knowledge, more battles, and, of course, more adventure!

ALL ABOUT ULTRA BEASTS

ULTRA BEASTS

According to the Legend of Solgaleo, many moons ago, unusual creatures from another world appeared: Ultra Beasts. These Ultra Beasts did not come in peace—they waged a war against the four Island Guardians. Solgaleo is said to have torn open the sky and then traveled through the tear to step in. The epic fight took place on Poni Island at the Altar of the Sunne. The battle was so brutal, it became a legend retold throughout Alola. Many believe that some Ultra Beasts may still be wandering Alola.

ULTRA AURA

Ultra Aura is an energy that is emitted from any physical element that comes from the world of the Ultra Beasts. The lab at the Aether Foundation closely monitors and measures Ultra Aura. When the reading jumps, they snap into action.

ULTRA GUARDIANS

It is the duty of Ultra Guardians to capture Ultra Beasts and return them to their home world or care for them in this one. Their job is of utmost importance to the safety and tranquility of the people of Alola. So the Aether Foundation has recruited brave Ultra Guardians like Ash, Kiawe, Lana, Sophocles, and Lillie!

ULTRA WORMHOLES

When there is a warp in the space-time continuum, a pathway opens between this world and the world of the Ultra Beasts. This temporary tunnel can pose a danger to both people and Pokémon, since Ultra Beasts have incredible power. So, researchers at the Aether Foundation constantly monitor Ultra Aura, looking for spikes in readings that could predict the opening of an Ultra Wormhole.

THE AETHER FOUNDATION

Housed at the Aether Paradise, this unique institution has two missions that are important to the protection of people and Pokémon. First, its staff and lab are devoted to research about Ultra Beasts and Ultra Wormholes. Second, the Aether Foundation runs an awesome Pokémon conservatory.

THE AETHER PARADISE

This incredible man-made island is stationed in the middle of the sea. Inside the massive facility is a Pokémon habitat that feels so much like the great outdoors, it's hard to believe it is entirely indoors. Pokémon from all over the world—every corner of every region—come here for special care. Whether a Pokémon is lost from its friends or is injured, the Aether Paradise will help them recover before being released back into the wild.

THE AETHER FOUNDATION STAFF

LUSAMINE: Lillie's mom, and president of the Aether Foundation.

PROFESSOR BURNET: The leading scientist focused on Ultra Wormholes.

WICKE: The chief of the Aether Foundation.

FABA: The Aether Foundation's branch chief. He can't be trusted because of his ambition and jealousy of Professor Burnet's success, but he is the scientist who created the mighty Silvally.

GLADION: Lusamine's son—Lillie's brother. He prefers to work independently on the same mission with his stolen Pokémon pal, Silvally.

POIPOLE

Poipole, one of the mysterious Ultra Beasts, is crowned with needles that spray a dangerous poison. This creature lives in another world, where it is popular enough that it could be a first partner.

NAGANADEL

Naganadel, one of the mysterious Ultra Beasts, stores a poisonous liquid in vast quantities inside its body. The poison, which gives off an eerie glow and adheres to anything it touches, can be fired from its needles.

STAKATAKA

It's thought that Stakataka, one of the mysterious Ultra Beasts, is made up of several life-forms stacked on top of one another. This creature resembles a stone wall covered with markings that look like blue eyes.

BLACEPHALON

Blacephalon, one of the mysterious Ultra Beasts, has an unexpected method of attack: it makes its own head blow up! Its opponents are so surprised by this that it can take advantage and steal their energy.

NIHILEGO

Nihilego, one of the mysterious Ultra Beasts, can apparently infest other beings and incite them to violence. Research is inconclusive as to whether this Pokémon can think for itself, but it sometimes exhibits the behavior of a young girl.

BUZZWOLE

Buzzwole, one of the mysterious Ultra Beasts, is enormously strong, capable of demolishing heavy machinery with a punch. When it displays its impressive muscles, no one is sure whether it's just showing off—or issuing a threat.

PHERMOSA

Pheromosa, one of the mysterious Ultra Beasts, seems to be extremely wary of germs and won't touch anything willingly. Witnesses have seen it charging through the region at amazing speeds.

XURKITREE

Xurkitree, one of the mysterious Ultra Beasts, invaded an electric plant after it emerged from the Ultra Wormhole. Some suspect it absorbs electricity into its body to power the serious shocks it gives off.

CELESTEELA

Celesteela, one of the mysterious Ultra Beasts, can shoot incendiary gases from its arms and has been known to burn down wide swaths of trees. In flight, it can reach impressive speeds.

KARTANA

Kartana, one of the mysterious Ultra Beasts, can use its entire sharp-edged body as a weapon in battle. Its blade is strong and sharp enough to slice right through a steel structure in a single stroke.

GUZZLORD

Guzzlord, one of the mysterious Ultra Beasts, seems to have an insatiable appetite for just about everything—it will even swallow buildings and mountains. This constant munching can be very destructive.

Ash and his friends have had some pretty amazing battles in Alola. Here are a few highlights.

ASH VS. KAHUNA HALA

Ash faced off against Kahuna Hala in his first grand trial. Round one featured Ash and Rowlet against Hala and Crabrawler. Although Rowlet sealed a win, it was so tired from the epic fight that it fell asleep in midair! Next, Hala chose the powerful Pokémon Hariyama, and Ash called on Pikachu. Hala unleashed the Fighting-type Z-Move, All-Out Pummeling—but thanks to Quick Attack, Pikachu dodged every hit. Ash used the Z-Move Breakneck Blitz to win the grand trial!

ASH VS. THE MASKED ROYAL

While watching TV, Ash discovered the Battle Royal. The star of the show is the Masked Royal and his Pokémon partner Incineroar, and the game features four Pokémon who battle until there is only one left standing. Ash immediately challenged the Masked Royal with his friends Kiawe and Sophocles, but the Masked Royal defeated them all. However, Litten wanted to battle again the next day. During the rematch, Litten evolved into Torracat! (And in an even bigger surprise, the Masked Royal is secretly actually Professor Kukui in disguise!)

LEGENDARY POKÉMON OF ALOLA

COSMOG

Cosmog reportedly came to the Alola region from another world, but its origins are shrouded in mystery. Known as the child of the stars, it grows by gathering dust from the atmosphere.

COSMOEM

Cosmoem never moves, radiating a gentle warmth as it develops inside the hard shell that surrounds it. Long ago, people referred to it as the cocoon of the stars, and some still think its origins lie in another world.

SOLGALEO

Solgaleo's entire body radiates a bright light that can wipe away the darkness of night. This Legendary Pokémon apparently makes its home in another world, and it returns there when its third eye becomes active.

LUNALA

Lunala's wide wings soak up the light, plunging the brightest day into shadow. This Legendary Pokémon apparently makes its home in another world, and it returns there when its third eye becomes active.

NECROZMA

Some think Necrozma arrived from another world many eons ago. When it emerges from its underground slumber, it seems to absorb light for use as energy to power its laser-like blasts.

TAPU BULU

Tapu Bulu has a reputation for laziness—rather than battling directly, it commands vines to pin down its foes. The plants that grow abundantly in its wake give it energy. It's known as the guardian of Ula'ula Island.

TAPU FINI

Tapu Fini can control and cleanse water, washing away impurities. When threatened, it summons a dense fog to confuse its enemies. This Pokémon draws energy from ocean currents. It's known as the guardian of Poni Island.

TAPU LELE

As Tapu Lele flutters through the air, people in search of good health gather up the glowing scales that fall from its body. It draws energy from the scent of flowers. It's known as the guardian of Akala Island.

TAPU KOKO

Somewhat lacking in attention span, Tapu Koko is quick to anger but just as quickly forgets why it's angry. Calling thunderclouds lets it store up lightning as energy. It's known as the guardian of Melemele Island.

TYPE: NULL

The synthetic Pokémon known as Type: Null wears a heavy mask to keep its power in check. Some fear that without the mask, it would lose control of its powers and go on a destructive rampage.

SILVALLY

Learning to trust its Trainer caused this Pokémon to evolve and discard the mask that kept its power tightly controlled. Silvally can change its type in battle, making it a formidable opponent.

MYTHICAL POKEMON OF ALOLA

MARSHADOW

Very few people have seen Marshadow, so it was considered a rumor. Always cowering in the shadows, it watches others closely and mimics their movements.

MAGEARNA

Magearna was built many centuries ago by human inventors. The rest of this Pokémon's mechanical body is just a vehicle for its true self: the Soul-Heart contained in its chest.

ZERAORA

Zeraora electrifies its claws and tears its opponents apart with them. Even if they dodge its attack, they'll be electrocuted by the flying sparks.

POKÉMON VS. ALOLA POKÉMON

In Alola, Ash encounters some Pokémon that make him do a double take. They sure look like Pokémon he's met, but something has changed. Ash soon learns that the Alolan Pokémon can look similar to Pokémon species he's familiar with, but they can be very different—possibly even a different type.

According to Principal Samson Oak, some Pokémon can develop a distinct appearance based on the region in which they live. For example, the reason the Alolan Exeggutor have grown taller is Alola's year-round warm and sunny climate.

DIGLETT
Height: 0'08"
Weight: 1.8 lbs.
Type: Ground

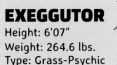

ALOLAN DIGLETT
Height: 0'08"
Weight: 2.2 lbs.
Type: Ground-Steel

DUGTRIO
Height: 2'04"
Weight: 73.4 lbs.
Type: Ground

ALOLAN DUGTRIO
Height: 2'04"
Weight: 146.8 lbs.
Type: Ground-Steel

EXEGGUTOR
Height: 6'07"
Weight: 264.6 lbs.
Type: Grass-Psychic

ALOLAN EXEGGUTOR
Height: 35'09"
Weight: 916.2 lbs.
Type: Grass-Dragon

GEODUDE
Height: 1'04"
Weight: 44.1 lbs.
Type: Rock-Ground

ALOLAN GEODUDE
Height: 1'04"
Weight: 44.8 lbs.
Type: Rock-Electric

GOLEM
Height: 4'07"
Weight: 661.4 lbs
Type: Rock-Ground

ALOLAN GOLEM
Height: 5'07"
Weight: 696.7 lbs.
Type: Rock-Electric

GRAVELER
Height: 3'03"
Weight: 231.5 lbs.
Type: Rock-Ground

ALOLAN GRAVELER
Height: 3'03"
Weight: 242.5 lbs.
Type: Rock-Electric

GRIMER
Height: 2'11"
Weight: 66.1 lbs.
Type: Poison

ALOLAN GRIMER
Height: 2'04"
Weight: 92.6 lbs.
Type: Poison-Dark

MAROWAK
Height: 3'03"
Weight: 99.2 lbs.
Type: Ground

ALOLAN MAROWAK
Height: 3'03"
Weight: 75.0 lbs.
Type: Fire-Ghost

MEOWTH
Height: 1'04"
Weight: 9.3 lbs.
Type: Normal

ALOLAN MEOWTH
Height: 1'04"
Weight: 9.3 lbs.
Type: Dark

MUK
Height: 3'11"
Weight: 66.1 lbs.
Type: Poison

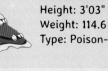

ALOLAN MUK
Height: 3'03"
Weight: 114.6 lbs.
Type: Poison-Dark

NINETALES
Height: 3'07"
Weight: 43.9 lbs.
Type: Fire

ALOLAN NINETALES
Height: 3'07"
Weight: 43.9 lbs.
Type: Ice-Fairy

PERSIAN

Height: 3'03"
Weight: 70.5 lbs.
Type: Normal

ALOLAN PERSIAN

Height: 3'07"
Weight: 72.8 lbs.
Type: Dark

RAICHU

Height: 2'07"
Weight: 66.1 lbs.
Type: Electric

ALOLAN RAICHU

Height: 2'04"
Weight: 46.3 lbs.
Type: Electric-Psychic

RATICATE

Height: 2'04"
Weight: 40.8 lbs.
Type: Normal

ALOLAN RATICATE

Height: 2'04"
Weight: 56.2 lbs.
Type: Dark-Normal

RATTATA

Height: 1'00"
Weight: 7.7 lbs.
Type: Normal

ALOLAN RATTATA

Height: 1'00"
Weight: 8.4 lbs.
Type: Dark-Normal

SANDSHREW

Height: 2'00"
Weight: 26.5 lbs.
Type: Ground

ALOLAN SANDSHREW

Height: 2'04"
Weight: 88.2 lbs.
Type: Ice-Steel

SANDSLASH

Height: 3'03"
Weight: 65.0 lbs.
Type: Ground

ALOLAN SANDSLASH
Height: 3'11"
Weight: 121.3 lbs.
Type: Ice-Steel

VULPIX

Height: 2'00"
Weight: 21.8 lbs.
Type: Fire

ALOLAN VULPIX

Height: 2'00"
Weight: 21.8 lbs.
Type: Ice

CONCLUSION

Ash's quest has lead him from Kanto to Johto to Hoenn to Sinnoh to Unova to Kalos to Alola . . . but this is just the beginning! Who knows where his curiosity and dedication will take him next? His journey to become a Pokémon Master continues!

One thing's for sure: Wherever Ash goes, adventure follows. And, of course, he's hoping all his friends—including you and Pikachu—are ready for more!